The WICKED MARQUIS

The WICKED MARQUIS

— Marnie Ellingson —

WALKER AND COMPANY
NEW YORK

First published in the United States of America
in 1982 by the Walker Publishing Company, Inc.

Published simultaneously in Canada by John Wiley & Sons Canada,
Limited, Rexdale, Ontario.

ISBN: 0-8027-0707-6

Library of Congress Catalog Card Number: 81-71915

Printed in the United States of America

10 9 8 7 6 5 4 3 2 1

=1=

WHEN THE WHEELS of the gig heralded its arrival by
crunching over the gravel drive in front of Wellspring House,
three fair heads poked out of an upstairs window. Three pairs
of interested eyes watched as the groom handed his passenger
down.

"She looks very short," Constance said, "or is it only from
this angle?"

"That's a delectable hat she's wearing," Hope said, rather
in awe.

Drusilla, the eldest, protested, "I don't see how that can
be our Cousin Esme after all—in a cherry red pelisse and her
papa scarcely six months dead!"

"But that's our gig and our groom. Why should he have
fetched anyone other than our cousin home from the coach
stop?" Constance wondered.

"Well, let's go and see," Hope said practically, and the
three heads drew in. Hands tidied hair and dress, then the
three sisters assumed poses of dignity before descending the
stairs.

On entering the morning room, they saw the stranger in
the cherry pelisse enfolded in the mama's plump arms and
realised that no matter the shade of her costume, she must
indeed be their cousin Esme Leonardo.

Lady Channing had drawn back now, holding her niece's
face between her hands, and was saying mistily, "I think
you do have a little look of dearest Estella despite your

colouring." Then, catching sight of her daughters, she cried, "Girls, come in and meet your cousin Esme! Esme, my eldest daughter Drusilla, then Hope, and my baby Constance."

Since Constance was very nearly fifteen, she was nettled to hear herself termed "baby" in front of her exotic cousin, but she made a very pretty curtsey despite feeling aggrieved.

Drusilla studied the newcomer, who was about her own age, and judged at once that the masses of dark hair that could be seen beneath the brim of the fetching bonnet had never needed the touch of a curl-paper. Her dark eyes were enormous. Her nose was perhaps a shade too short and her mouth a bit too wide; still, she had a very lively look about her. She was indeed, as Constance had commented, not of the statuesque height and form which was the current ideal of beauty, but if one were speaking charitably, her figure could be termed dainty rather than insignificant. Her complexion, inherited no doubt from her Italian father, was hardly peaches-and-cream; it was more of a pale olive, as if she had been careless about protecting it from the sun.

On the whole, Drusilla thought her quite pretty in a foreign sort of way, though certainly not ravishing, and was well pleased with her appearance. If one were accustomed to being considered the prettiest girl in the neighbourhood, one would not wish for one's cousin to be an antidote, but one would have to be unselfish to the point of saintliness to wish for an Incomparable to be deposited in the midst of one's social set and to be obliged to take her to one's bosom. Drusilla did not think she would have any difficulty taking Esme to her bosom.

"Hope, ring for tea," her mama directed, and led Esme tenderly to a place beside her on a sofa. "I can scarcely believe it: My dear sister's child with me after all these years." She wiped her eyes.

"It is so good of you to have me, Aunt," Esme said. Her voice had a slightly husky, though not unpleasant, quality. "I hope my coming will not discommode you too much, or my Uncle Frederick either."

"Oh no, how could you think it!" Lady Channing exclaimed.

"Well, he will probably be shocked that you are not in mourning," Constance said frankly, earning herself a confused frown from her mama, who recognised the force of the statement but deplored her daughter's lack of tact.

"Oh, *Papa* did not believe in long mourning," Esme said, not at all discomfited. "He liked bright colours, which was a very good thing as he had to spend so much of his time in costume, you know. *Papa* said—"

She broke off as her aunt gave a perceptible quiver. "What is it, Aunt Dora? Have I said something wrong?"

After an uncomfortable pause, Lady Channing nerved herself. "My dear child, you will *not*, I think, believe I have any wish to criticise, but if only I could drop the tiniest hint. . . . It is best to begin as we mean to go on, do you not agree?"

"Why, yes," Esme replied, puzzled.

"It is only that it will be so much more comfortable if you are not forever quoting your papa. You see, your Uncle Frederick never quite forgave your papa, I fear, for marrying our sainted sister and—"

Here Esme burst out in a peal of laughter. "Sainted? Mama? Why, she was as full of mischief as could hold together. You could hardly credit the jolly times we had."

"Yes, well, that's as may be, but when she married to disoblige her family, and your papa took her off to the Continent and never brought her back again—"

"But that was because of the horrid war, of course," Esme interrupted, "and anyway, he did bring her back once when I was quite a child."

"Yes, yes." Lady Channing shuddered faintly, remembering. Estella's husband, a noted opera singer, had come once to London on a triumphal tour, but Estella had refused to leave him to come into the country to visit Frederick, and her brother had refused to go next or nigh London "to see that damned foreigner prancing around in tights." Lady Channing *had* gone up to London and had heard him sing

7

and thought that "prancing" was scarcely the right word for his majestic stage presence. Also, since the opera was about a desert sheik, if he had been wearing tights, they had been well concealed under his burnoose, but there was no use at all in mentioning such a point to Frederick once he took a notion into his head. Or in telling him that Estella seemed embarrassingly happy with her lot in life. Actually, Lady Channing had rather liked her brother-in-law—or thought she would have, had she had time to accustom herself to his expansive manners.

The arrival of the tea put a temporary halt to her admonitions to Esme, but when it had been poured out, she went on. "I do realise that your papa wasn't responsible for Bonaparte; still, he did take your mama away, and your uncle could never really rid himself of a feeling of ill usage. He has a great sense of duty, you see, and I will say he has always done his duty by me, so when your mama refused to marry the gentleman *our* papa had picked out for her—and there's no denying that the marriage would have been of the greatest benefit to the family—but insisted on an opera singer instead, well, you can imagine his feelings."

"I see," Esme said with a worried frown, setting her cup down. "Then perhaps he doesn't want me here at all. I daresay I can contrive something else."

"Oh no, no! You mustn't think such a thing. He doesn't blame *you* in the least, and as I said, he has a strong sense of duty. Only look at the way he took me and my brood in when my poor Hubert died. He could scarcely do less for his other sister's child. No, he is very content for you to be here; it is only that I felt I should warn you that he will not be pleased to hear very much reminiscing about your papa's views. And perhaps something a little more conservative in the way of dress."

"I don't have mourning clothes," Esme said and then brightened. "I know! I shall tell him I couldn't afford any."

Her aunt regarded her uneasily. She could not be happy to hear Esme so willing to tell an untruth, and to say so in front of her cousins, but perhaps any explanation would be better than having her quote Signor Leonardo's views on mourning—or rather, the lack of it. And on further reflection she comforted herself with the thought that perhaps indeed Esme had *not* had the money to buy mourning garb, so it would not be a falsehood to say so.

Upstairs in the dainty yellow room to which Esme's boxes had been taken, the three Channing girls settled themselves in to watch their cousin finish her unpacking, which had been only partially completed by a maid. Her dresses had been hung in the wardrobe, but one trunk was still half-full of the most extraordinary treasures: feathers and lengths of spangled gauze, Honiton lace and silk braid.

Constance pounced upon a spray of velvet forget-me-nots. "Gracious, Esme, whatever will you do with all these things?"

Esme took the spray and fashioned it into a circlet. "Why, this I'll give to you to wear in your hair to a ball. *Mi permetta.*" And she placed it on Constance's fair curls. "Blue becomes you much better than me, with your blonde hair."

"She's much too young for balls," Hope said scornfully.

"And so are you," Constance retorted. "Dru is the only one of us who's out yet, and she's not fully out, of course, but only out in the neighbourhood."

"But I shall have my come-out next Season in London," Drusilla declared, "if Mama can contrive it."

"But what are all these delicious things for?" Constance repeated, snubbing her sister's pretensions at being a debutante.

"Waste not, want not," Esme quoted. "Who knows when they'll come in handy? I expect I shall have to make my own clothes, you know, and that is one thing I am quite good at. I learned ever so many useful things from Papa's costumière, and she was used to give me all manner of bits and pieces. Luckily, I know how to refashion and trim a gown so it can hardly be recognised."

"Are you quite destitute then?" Constance asked.

9

"Connie! Don't be rude," her eldest sister reproved, though Drusilla was quite as interested in Esme's financial situation as the younger girls, as it was a subject which had been discussed by her mother and uncle only behind closed doors.

"Not quite destitute, though my competence is meagre enough that I cannot look for an advantageous marriage," Esme said practically. "I have thought I might set up as a modiste when I am a little older."

"Oh, but surely you must marry," Hope cried, "if you are not quite penniless. After all, you are a baronet's grand-daughter on your mama's side, and that ought to count for something, even if your papa *was* Italian and a singer."

Drusilla cast her a repressive look. "But of a very good Italian family, Mama has always said."

"But your papa was a *famous* singer. I thought he made pots of money," Constance said.

"Don't be vulgar," Dru said, but not very forcefully, as she was hoping to hear more of her cousin's story.

"Oh, he did until three years ago when Mama died. You see, they were sailing, and their boat overturned. They both fell ill of an inflammation of the lungs, and Mama died. Papa recovered, but his voice was affected. Perhaps it would have come back, but he was stricken with grief and didn't really care to go on without Mama. Without her, and being unable to sing, he felt there was nothing to live for, no excitement in his life, so he took to gambling and drinking brandy. Unhappily, he wasn't very good at either since he had never practised at it before."

"But how awful for you!" Drusilla said.

"Yes, I miss him very much, but I quite understood how it was. Papa was always very volatile, and he adored Mama to the point of distraction." She spoke without rancour, though a less forgiving daughter might have been excused for wishing her papa had chosen to express his grief in some way less calculated to ruin his child as well as himself. "Luckily,

Mama had left a little legacy to me, and he couldn't gamble it away because the principal can't be touched till I'm one-and-twenty, so I do have a small income. And I have her pearls and a ruby pendant that she especially liked. Papa wouldn't have touched her jewels, of course, only I had to sell the rest of them to settle his debts. But I have some lovely swansdown from one of Mama's cloaks that will do very well to trim a pelisse, and heaps of seed pearls and diamante brilliants and silver leaves that I cut off some of her old gowns, so I shall contrive not to look like a dowd."

"Oh Esme," Drusilla said, much moved by this tale and her cousin's unaffected air in recounting it. "I do not think you could ever look like a dowd. You have too much natural style."

"Yes, I shouldn't be surprised if she should *take* very well," Hope said, aping the tone she had heard her elders use. "Besides, when Dru is married, very likely she can do something useful for you."

"Oh, are you betrothed then?" Esme asked her cousin with great interest.

"No, of course not," Dru said. "I haven't even had my Season."

"But we are hoping for great things," Hope said, "her looks being so especially fine, you know. She is the only one of us to have inherited the Channing nose, and I believe honey-coloured hair such as hers can never be despised. Besides, our papa was younger son to a marquis, and that must count for something, even if her portion will not be large."

"And then when our brother Kit succeeds to the title—" Constance began.

But Drusilla interrupted. "I should be quite on the shelf if I waited for that, since our cousin, the present marquis, is not *absolutely* in his dotage."

"But high living and dissipation take their toll," Hope said, again with the air of quoting overheard conversations. "Besides, he is likely to be killed in a duel, I should think."

"Oh my," Esme said. "I don't believe I have ever heard of the wicked marquis who is your cousin."

"I daresay not," Dru said, "as he is on the other side of the family, our papa's, you know. And now that my sisters have gossiped your ears off, we must leave you to your settling in. We dine at six, which is *not* what one would wish, but Uncle Frederick keeps country hours."

With that, they took their leave of her, Constance giving her an impulsive hug before they trooped out of the room.

Though the Channing girls were not in nearly such straitened circumstances as their cousin Esme, their degree of independence was a limited one, and they too were in a sense pensioners of their Uncle Frederick Hasborough.

Their mother had indeed married Hubert Channing, a son of the Marquis of Locklynde, quite a good match for the daughter of a minor baronet. Unfortunately, her husband was the youngest of a large brood. The bulk of the estate was of course entailed upon his eldest brother. By the time his prolific father had provided ample marriage settlements for four daughters, arranged an advantageous preferment for his second son who had gone into the church, bought an expensive army commission for his third son, and launched his fourth into a career in politics, his age was advanced and his purse depleted. His youngest offspring, Lord Hubert, who, in all fairness to his long-suffering father, showed no particular inclination for any other career, was thus given a tidy little estate in Wiltshire, along with his father's good wishes that he might settle down to the life of a country gentleman and make a profitable venture of his land.

Lord Hubert did manage to produce a son and three daughters, but along the way discovered that drainage ditches and silage could never hold his interest, and that raising cows could not compare to raising a splash among the high-fliers of London.

Perhaps the closest he approached to the ideal of a gentleman farmer was in his stables, which were crowded with the most expensive thoroughbred horses, the amount of money expended on them being somewhat in advance even of the cumulative cost of the baubles and gowns he showered on his succession of opera dancers and other inamorata. Luckily, an overturned curricle put a period to his existence before his pockets were entirely to let, and his widow found the only comforting point in the whole sad business to be the fact that the fatal curricle race took place when it did, and not a week later, for after the funeral she found among his effects a particularly fine diamond parure intended as a gift for his current light o' love. The sale of this piece, together with that of Lord Hubert's horses, provided a sum which, properly invested by one of her brothers-in-law on her behalf, gave her a modest income.

At the time, her son Christopher was far too young to be able to look after the farm, and the house with its complement of servants was expensive to keep up, so when her brother Sir Frederick offered her a home with him, she accepted gratefully. Their father had died some years previously, leaving his title and land to Frederick, and Lady Channing was pleased to return to the home of her childhood, which was only some forty miles from her late husband's estate. The latter was put into the hands of an honest, if unimaginative, land agent, and the house was let to a wealthy cit, providing an added income for the widow.

Life at Wellspring House was not unpleasant. Sir Frederick was agreeable to leave the running of the household in her hands. He had been married once, but his wife had proved not only frail but fickle. When she had expired, he had not been in a hurry to repeat the experiment of marriage, and was well suited to have his sister reign over his household.

Lady Channing was very little out of pocket by the arrangement, being obliged to pay only for her own and her children's clothes, their governess and tutor, Kit's curricle, and her personal maid. The remainder of the household expenses were borne by her brother, and in fact he occasionally bestowed a handsome enough gift on the girls to enable them to buy a new gown.

Esme now surveyed her own gowns hanging neatly in the wardrobe, and it was her impulse to don the jonquil jaconet muslin, which was one of her favourites but, recalling her aunt's concern about her having no mourning clothes, she prudently chose a rather dull green book muslin that she hoped would not be exceptionable.

Her Uncle Frederick was standing with his back to the fire in the drawing room when she finished her toilette and went in to him. He took her hands for a moment, then placed his on either side of her head, the better to look at her face. "Very unlike your mother in colouring, but I think you have a look of her about the mouth and in the spacing of the eyebrows, do you not agree, Dora?"

Sir Frederick chose to regard himself as a sentimental man, and ever since his sister Estella had died, he cherished the memory of his own fondness for her when he was a boy, quite overlooking his years of pique when she had overset the family equilibrium by all but running off with an opera singer. Sir Frederick was a man of medium height and, though younger than his sister—scarcely past his fortieth year—his hair was almost completely white. His skin, however, was a healthy-looking pink and his eyes a keen blue for all that they were somewhat shortsighted.

Esme made him her prettiest curtsey and a little speech of gratitude that was so charmingly graceful he seemed inclined to overlook her unfortunate complexion. However, his benign mood did not prevent him from observing the colour of her dress. "I see you are not in mourning," he announced gravely.

"No sir. You see, I could not afford a new wardrobe, Papa's debts being what they were, and the friends I stayed with while his poor affairs were tidied up had done so much for me already that I could hardly ask *them* to supply me with mourning clothes."

14

"No, but now that you are here—" he began, when she interrupted, "Well, of course now I would only need half mourning, but I hate to put you to the expense when you have been so kind as to offer me a home. Do you not think, since more than six months have passed, we might safely take the thought for the deed, especially as Papa died in another country?"

What *that* had to do with anything, Lady Channing could not imagine, as she listened to her niece try to talk round Frederick. Oddly, however, he seemed to recognise the force of the argument as a reasonable way out of the dilemma of being required to provide his niece with a new wardrobe in memoriam to a man of whom he had never approved. He was a man to do his duty, but when it necessitated a considerable outlay of capital, it was agreeable to discover that it was not really a duty after all.

Dinner passed very pleasantly, with Esme guarding her tongue against untoward comments about what "Papa said" and telling several charming anecdotes about her mother instead, which were bound to be well received.

2

WELLSPRING HOUSE AND its environs were a source of great interest to Esme, who had been raised in such different surroundings. Much to her cousins' amusement, she fell into raptures over the scrawniest duckling and the stupidest lamb, and she professed to find the countryside with its neat hedgerows charming beyond words.

"Though how she could when she has been to the Alps, I can't imagine," Hope said.

Esme told them that she had lived with her parents in a rather ugly house in Milan not far from La Scala, the great opera house where her father had sung, but that they had also had a small villa at Bellagio on Lake Como, where they had retired whenever her father was not performing. She had accompanied her parents on tours to other cities in Italy, and even to foreign countries whenever the progress of the war did not interfere with travelling.

She had not been entered in a school, but had had her own English governess who went everywhere with her. Miss Cobham had been a most superior woman, excelling in music and art. She had previously been headmistress of her own school in Chelsea. She had taken the position with the Leonardos to satisfy her longing to explore the Continent, and Italy in particular. Wherever they had journeyed, Cobbie had taken Esme to explore the museums, galleries, and cathedrals of the city while her father rehearsed. After Esme's mother had died and her papa had begun his ruinous course,

Miss Cobham had loyally stayed on for, as she said, she had had many happy years with them, enjoying all the advantages of travel and the opportunity to hear her beloved opera as often as she chose, and she would not desert her post now. She had stayed, in fact, as Esme's chaperone long enough to see her safely back to England.

Knowing that it had been Miss Cobham's plan to use her savings to open another school in England when her position with the Leonardos terminated, Esme had made sure that the first debt she discharged after her father's death was Cobbie's salary, which had gone unpaid for so long. Her governess had not wanted to take it, but Esme had insisted, carefully hiding from her the fact that some of her mother's jewels had gone to make up the sum. "For you know, Cobbie," she had said, "it is in my own interests that you open your school. Who knows but that I may have to come to you begging a position one day?"

The ladies at Wellspring House received a number of callers during the first week after Esme's arrival. A new resident was bound to be the object of curiosity in such a quiet neighbourhood. Opinion was somewhat divided on the newcomer. Those matrons who remembered the young Estella Hasborough with fondness pronounced Esme to be a very pretty-behaved girl. Several who had suffered in their girlhood by comparison with Estella's popularity found her daughter a little too *coming*. Among the younger ladies, Edith Brownlow—who was decidedly plain—pronounced Esme pert, while Amy Harris—who was also plain, but had a quick mind and pleasant disposition—found Esme both personable and clever. The more romantically inclined were eager to discuss life in Italy with her and were only disappointed that she was not personally acquainted with Lord Byron. They found her otherwise entertaining.

About ten days after she had joined the household, the rest of the family fell into a pleasant commotion over the return of Christopher from a few weeks spent at Tydings. He was not long down from Oxford and was trying to get the feel of running his farm and dealing with his modest number of tenants, against the day when he would be able to establish himself on the place.

Constance promised Esme an especially good dinner for, as she said, "Cook fairly dotes on Kit." Esme noticed that Kit's mother and all three of his sisters had made themselves especially smart, and thought perhaps they all doted on him. She wondered if he could help being spoiled by all this attention. For some perverse reason she could not define, she chose to wear her rather drab green dress that evening, and dressed her hair simply and confined it with a ribbon.

Kit had arrived home and gone to his bedchamber to change for dinner without her laying eyes on him, and now she found herself alone in the drawing room before dinner. Suddenly she heard a voice behind her. "Well, good evening. You must be my little cousin Esme!"

She spun around, a haughty remark rising to her lips, and found herself looking up at quite the handsomest young man she had ever seen. His gold hair tumbled casually over a fine, high forehead. His eyes were a deep blue. His chin was firm, his cheeks high-planed, and his mouth was now curved in an irresistible smile of welcome. She found herself stammering slightly as she held out her hand to him.

"I hope my sisters are taking good care of you. You must find this countryside very tame and quiet after the splendours of Milan."

"Oh no, not at all," she said, and then blushed as she realised what a stupid remark it was. "Well, of course it is quieter, but I like it extremely, and your sisters have been all that is kind."

"I hope you have not let them choose a horse for you. The three of them together haven't the judgement of a quarter-wit when it comes to horseflesh, though they ride tolerably. But they are forever wanting to choose a horse by its colour or by some touching expression they fancy they see on its face."

"The question of horses hasn't yet arisen, but I suppose I

should do the same," Esme admitted. "I haven't ridden for several years—not since my mama died."

"Well, you must let me find you a mount. I remember Dru plaguing Uncle Frederick to buy a roan stallion for her because she thought he looked *wistful*. He was the worst bolter in the county and had a trick of taking a fence three times smooth as butter and then stopping dead the fourth time, hoping to break his rider's neck. Wistful!" His eyes crinkled up with an amusement that was so infectious it made Esme laugh.

"How does it happen you speak English without an accent?" he asked. "You spent all your life in Italy, did you not?"

"Yes, but my governess was English, and Mama always spoke English to me. In fact, she and Papa usually spoke to each other in English, and we had a good many guests from this country."

"Kit! I see you've met Esme," his mama said, coming into the room followed by her brother.

"My boy, it's good to have you back," Sir Frederick said. "After dinner, we shall have to have a long talk about how you found your acres."

During the repast, Kit caught his mother up on all the news he had gleaned of her old neighbours. "Oh, and the Bottikins have repainted the drawing room. A rather horrible dirty pink, actually. Mrs. Bottikin invited me to take my mutton with them one night." He made a wry grimace. The Bottikins were the cits who were renting the house at Tydings. "I must admit Mr. Bottikin has laid in some good claret."

Esme neither knew nor cared about any of the people he was discussing, but it was pleasant to listen to his voice and watch him as he spoke. It was agreeable to have a masculine presence in the house other than Sir Frederick's, whose personality, it must be admitted, was less invigourating than his nephew's.

Suddenly it occurred to her to wonder how it was that she

19

had neglected to mention to Kit that she could not afford to buy a horse. She would have to repair the omission before he went to the trouble of searching one out for her.

As a tray of creams was carried in, he brought up the subject himself. "I'm going to find a horse for Esme tomorrow. Do you know if Peters still has that dapple mare, sir?"

"Oh," Esme said, "I have realised since we talked earlier that until next quarter day I really could not think of such a purchase, but possibly at that time—"

"Nonsense," her uncle interrupted. "I shall provide you with a mount. You're a country girl now. You must have a horse."

"Oh, Uncle Frederick!" She was quite overcome. "You are—" She stopped suddenly and choked back the words *molto generoso*, as she remembered he did not like to be reminded of the Italian part of her heritage, and finished tamely, "You are so very kind to me."

"I provided your cousins with mounts. I can't have it said that I didn't do my duty by my other niece," he said, somewhat diminishing her feeling of acute gratitude.

The next morning Dru was in her room when Esme dug out her old riding habit and held it up to herself. "It's a good thing I attained my full height early. This will still fit me, I think."

It was a bottle green velvet and was rather shabby at the cuffs and closures. Dru tried not to look at the worn spots, but said, "What a pretty colour."

"I know it's seen better days," Esme admitted frankly, "but I can cover up the frayed places with braid and trim it *à la militaire*." The green plume for her hat was quite hopelessly bedraggled, but she dug into her bandbox of bits and pieces and found some iridescent black coq feathers, which she substituted.

True to his word, Kit brought home a mare for her inspection. She was a dainty little dapple grey, and Esme loved her on sight. "What is her name?" she asked, nuzzling the velvet nose.

His face took on a pained expression. "I'm afraid it's Peaseblossom, but you may call her anything you like."

"Oh no. if I change her name, she might not know who she is any longer, and it would change her personality, too."

Kit laughed. "It's very nice having you here, Esme, almost like a new-found sister." He pulled one of her curls with careless affection.

If something twisted ever so slightly in her heart, it was only for a moment, and then she smiled up at her handsome cousin. If he wanted her for a sister, a sister she would be. "Well, I have always thought it would be quite marvellous to have a brother," she told him sincerely, and put all thoughts of something else behind her.

Later in the day, as they finished tea, Lady Channing said, "Here is some news that will interest you, girls. The Millimans are home from Exeter and are holding a rout party on Friday, and they have included Esme in the invitation. It will be her first outing of that nature in the neighbourhood. I'm sure she will enjoy it excessively."

Esme was quite ready to be pleased with the invitation and only regretted that Hope and Constance were too young to attend. They did not seem to be much cast down over having to miss the festivities, but Esme was so preoccupied over what to wear that she scarcely noticed.

She finally decided upon the yellow jaconet, which had a high waist, tiny puffed sleeves, and a moderately low neckline, its only trimming a very pretty braid twisted with seed pearls. She and Drusilla made a striking pair: the one so dark, the other so fair.

She could not help feeling rather excited as her uncle handed her into his big, old-fashioned carriage. He was looking quite fine tonight, with an ornate gold-and-pearl stickpin in his neckcloth, and he seemed in high good humour. She gathered from his conversation that he and Mr. Milliman were old cronies and that there was no household in the neighbourhood that he would be more pleased to visit

Drusilla seemed most eager to discover whether the new dress she was wearing would prove as successful as she hoped, and she and her mother held an animated discussion concerning the depth of the flounce. Only Kit was silent, staring fixedly out of the window and, when spoken to, answering in so abstracted a manner that Esme could not help wondering at it. It crossed her mind that he must be suffering from some trifling ailment like the headache, to be in this glum humour that was so unlike him.

The large, square Milliman house was lighted from top to bottom as the Channings' carriage drew up in the drive and the footman let down the steps.

Esme's quick eyes glanced around the entrance hall and saw that it was expensively, if not very pleasingly, appointed. She saw also, with pleasure, a number of the neighbours who had previously called at Wellspring House, including the charming Lady Dartney, who had been one of her mama's bosom bows.

Then she found herself at the top of the staircase, being greeted by her host and hostess and their daughter Lydia. Mrs. Milliman had an imposing figure, which was not very becomingly arrayed in puce sarcenet. Her daughter was of a bit more than average height, with brown hair dressed in elaborate poufs. She was wearing pink gauze over white satin—a little dressy for a rout party. Upon being introduced, she looked down at Esme and said, "I'm sorry Mama and I were unable to call upon you earlier. We have only just returned three days ago from a visit to my aunt, Lady Osbald."

"It was kind of you to invite me tonight," Esme said politely.

"Mama and I were quite at a stand to know whether you would be offended at being asked out in society so soon after your loss, but I see we need not have scrupled," she said, eyeing Esme's gown with a little lift of her brows, "since you do not observe mourning."

"Oh, my mourning period is over," Esme stated unequivocally.

"Really?" Lydia's brows rose higher. "I should not have thought that possible so soon."

"Perhaps you have been misinformed as to the date of my father's demise," Esme said firmly. "It took the news some time to reach England, I believe, and perhaps even a little longer to make the rounds of the neighbourhood."

As she passed on to make way for other newcomers, she reflected that it was odd the way Miss Milliman's manner had grated upon her. Was it Lydia's implied criticism of her dress? Lydia's features were not precisely displeasing, except for her teeth which, though very white, were too large for her rather pursed little mouth. But her high forehead was furrowed with creases, as if her brows were continually raised in surprise at the foibles of her acquaintance. Esme and Lydia were much of an age, and since the Millimans were such close neighbours, Esme had hoped they would be friends. Now she wondered. And yet surely it was unfair to form an aversion on so slight an acquaintance.

Esme had not intended to dance that evening, but after having mendaciously informed Lydia that her mourning period was over, she had no excuse for not doing so. And it was not quite mendacious, after all, for though the year was not up, the last thing her papa would have wished was for her to sustain a protracted period of grief, and so when a very pleasant young man whom she had met a few days earlier asked her to stand up with him for a country set, she agreed after only the tiniest hesitation and soon found that she was enjoying herself very much.

Dru also seemed to be having a good time carrying on an animated conversation with her partner whenever the figures of the dance allowed it. But when Esme caught sight of Kit, she hardly recognised him. He was going through the steps with Lydia Milliman in so stiff a way, his face so white and set, that he might have been a waxwork figure. Where were his laughing good looks, his easy grace? She began to fear he must indeed be ill.

Shortly after the set had ended, however, she saw that he was conversing amiably, if without much enthusiasm, with a group of other young men, and later he claimed Esme's hand for a set. She found him a very graceful dancer—as she would have expected him to be until she had observed his wooden performance of half an hour before. Perhaps if he had had the headache, he was feeling better now. With some lively nonsense, she was even able to coax a hint of laughter into his handsome eyes.

She soon observed that her cousin Dru was a popular girl in the neighbourhood, perhaps as much because of her charming, easy manners as because of her beauty.

For her own part, Esme was pleased to have her hand sought for enough dances that she need not feel like a wallflower, and yet she was perfectly happy to spend part of her time conversing with Lady Dartney and some of the other ladies who had called upon her, and with Amy Harris, whose unpretentious wit was very much to Esme's liking.

Mr. Milliman was condescending enough to pass a few words with her, congratulating her on her good fortune at finding a home in so felicitous a neighbourhood after suffering the rigours of exile in foreign parts.

A picture of her parents' delightful villa overlooking the turquoise waters of Lake Como flitted through Esme's mind and almost overset her gravity at his use of the word "rigours," but the past three years had told quite a different story indeed, and she kept her countenance and agreed with him sincerely that the Wiltshire countryside was pleasing beyond anything and that her aunt and uncle had been all that was kind.

It was apparent that no expense had been spared in providing a groaning board of delicacies for the supper that followed the dancing and card-playing.

Afterward Mrs. Milliman said, with a rather arch expression, "Perhaps Miss Leonardo would favour us with a few songs. I'm sure she must be very musical."

Esme laughed. "Oh dear. I'm afraid I have a voice like a crow. Even my father, loving as he was, could not countenance wasting a singing teacher's time on *me*."

Mrs. Milliman did not look particularly cast down by this intelligence but turned expectantly to her daughter. "I'm sure then that Lydia will oblige, will you not, my love?"

"Of course, Mama, but I will need someone to turn the pages," Lydia said. "If Mr. Channing would be so kind. . . ."

Poor Kit stammered out an almost incoherent reply to the effect that he could scarcely read a note. He appeared so stricken that Esme took pity on him and said quickly, "I'll be happy to accompany you; then you won't need anyone to turn the pages."

Lydia cast her a furious look. "I'm afraid you are not familiar with my music."

"Oh, that doesn't signify," Esme said carelessly. "I daresay I shall be able to read it well enough," and she seated herself at the pianoforte before any more objections could be raised.

Lydia turned her back to the assemblage and spent a long time sorting through her music. At last she handed a sheet to Esme with a spitefully triumphant little gleam. It was a quick, lively air, and Esme struck the opening bars with verve. But as Lydia began to sing, she increased the tempo until the words were hardly distinguishable, and Esme's fingers were fairly flying over the keyboard in order to keep up. She wondered what on earth Lydia was about; however, she did not falter, and finished quite nonchalantly to look up at the now panting, red-faced Lydia.

There was a moment of rather stunned silence, and then the audience applauded. "Perhaps you would like to try a slower piece this time," Esme suggested sweetly in a low tone. "I believe you must be out of breath."

25

The remainder of Lydia's selections were of a more moderate tempo, but when she had finished, to Esme's surprise, she found that the greater number of admiring compliments were reserved for her playing.

"My dear," Lady Dartney said, "I had no notion you were such a talented musician. You play beautifully."

"Oh, that was nothing," she said off-hand. "I had lessons since I was scarcely out of leading strings, and was forever accompanying my father."

"But you have a great gift."

"Oh no," she protested. "It is all virtuosity—mere technical accomplishment. A real musician feels it in his heart and soul. I'm much too prosaic."

"Perhaps, but your playing takes the shine out of everyone in these parts."

"I believe Miss Esme has not learned that false modesty can be an offense," Lydia said with a prim twitch of her head.

"Indeed I do recognise it as such," Esme said, "but when you are surrounded since birth as I was by the very finest musicians, you learn to tell the difference between first- and second-rate, and I definitely fall into the latter category."

There were two spots of colour high on Lydia's cheeks. "If you say so," she said. "What an elevating thing for the neighbourhood to have an expert at hand to rate our homely little performances."

"Oh, I listen to music only for the pleasure it brings," Esme said. "Believe me, I would never try to categorise *your* singing."

Fortunately, at that moment the butler announced that some of the carriages were at the door, and the party began to break up. On the ride home, Esme was conscious of two things—that she had somehow managed to make an enemy of Lydia Milliman, and that Kit had sunk once more into gloom, staring blankly out at the shadowy landscape while Drusilla's eyes rested on him with a softness that looked like pity.

"Into bed with both of you now," Lady Channing told the girls when they arrived home. "If you begin to chatter now, you'll have Hope and Constance awake too, like as not."

They kissed her and obediently went off to their own rooms, but Esme resolved to ask Dru at the first opportunity what might be troubling Kit.

3

THE OPPORTUNITY TO question Dru did not come early the next day, for the ladies were to pay some morning calls directly after breakfast, a meal which Kit ate almost in silence with a sort of rigid hopelessness in his face.

Esme could not help gazing at him in a perplexed way until she caught Dru's eyes upon her; Dru gave a furtive little shake of the head as if to warn Esme not to ask if anything were amiss.

When the calls had been duly paid and the ladies of the household had partaken of a light nuncheon, Lady Channing went off to confer with the housekeeper and Esme herded her cousins into her room. She faced them. "Now tell me, what is the matter with Kit? He has been so odd ever since last night, and you were motioning me not to call attention to it, Dru. Is he in some sort of trouble?"

"It was having to go to the Millimans'," Dru said. "That always throws him into a fit of the dismals."

"You see, Kit has a secret sorrow," Hope put in dramatically.

"Oh dear."

"He's in love with a girl named Verena Gaylord," Dru said.

"And she wasn't invited to the Millimans'?" Esme asked.

"Well, of course she wasn't. She lives in London. But that's not it. Kit wouldn't be so silly as to go into the mopes just because Verena wasn't at a party."

"Then his sorrow is that Verena doesn't return his love?" Esme asked thoughtfully.

"Of course she loves him," Hope said sharply, as if it were treason to suggest that anyone favoured with his regard could resist loving their adored brother.

"Then her family disapproves," Esme suggested.

"Oh no, they like Kit quite well enough, though as he can't offer for her, they will be sure to compel her to accept another offer eventually." Dru's tone was dismal.

"These Gaylords," Esme said. "I suppose then that they aren't quite the thing—beneath him socially, like the Bottikins?"

"The Gaylords are a perfectly unexceptionable family," Hope said indignantly. "Very old. I believe their bloodline can be traced back to the Conqueror."

"They are very poor then?"

"The Gaylords? Certainly not. Oh, they don't have an *enormous* fortune, but they are very comfortably situated. Where do you come by these fanciful ideas, Esme?" Dru asked.

"I expect it's from seeing so many operas," Constance suggested.

"Well, actually most operas are more about strangling and stabbing and suicide," Esme said. "But, *non intendo*—I don't understand. If Verena loves him and her irreproachable family is reconciled to the match, then what is Kit's secret sorrow?"

"There can be no match," Dru said. "Kit will have to offer for Lydia Milliman. It has always been understood."

"By whom?" Esme demanded.

"By Uncle Frederick and Lydia's father."

"But that's perfectly gothic," Esme protested. "It sounds like something out of an old-fashioned novel."

"Well, you see, Mr. Milliman and Uncle Frederick have been friends from boyhood, and I think under any circumstances they would be pleased to unite their families, but there is more to it than that. Their lands run together. For years, Uncle Frederick has wished to purchase an acreage from Mr. Milliman in order to further some agricultural scheme of his. But it is a very choice piece of property, and Mr. Milliman does not wish to sell; however, he has agreed that it will make up part of Lydia's dowry. Of course, once they are married, Kit will allow Uncle Frederick to do as he wishes with the land. After all, our uncle has given us a home these many years."

Esme frowned. "But why is Mr. Milliman so set on the marriage?"

"Though he is quite well-to-do, he has no title. His sister married a baron and is now Lady Osbald, and Lydia's cousins are the Honourable Sarah and the Honourable Elizabeth. I think Lydia has always felt keenly the sting of being plain Miss Milliman when her cousins are Honourables, and I'm sure her mama feels herself more worthy of being a Lady than her sister-in-law, whom she considers frivolous. They are perfectly set on Lydia marrying a title, and as she is their only child and eventually will inherit their whole estate, it's not an unreasonable expectation, only—"

"—only she is certainly not good enough for Kit," Esme said indignantly.

Her cousins looked at each other helplessly. "She's not exactly ill-favoured," Dru said in the tone of someone trying hard to be fair.

"She's so *serious*," Constance said. "She never laughs and only allows herself a superior smile if she hears of someone else landing in the suds."

"So this explains why she looked daggers at me when I offered to accompany her last night and save Kit from having to turn the pages for her. I only did it because I thought he hadn't been feeling quite the thing and he looked so uncomfortable when she suggested it," Esme said, and then paused as further enlightenment came to her. "Why, how dreadful! Now I understand why she sang that first song so fast no one could make out the words. She was trying to make me stumble and show me up. What a horrid, spiteful girl! She won't do for Kit at all. Is Verena very lovely?''

"Oh, she's an angel—the dearest girl.''

Esme gave herself a little shake and unselfishly decided that if her splendid cousin wanted the angelic Verena, then he must have her.

"But how is it that Kit is to inherit a title?'' she asked. "You said something about it the other day.''

"Papa's father was the Marquis of Locklynde,'' Dru explained. "There were five sons altogether. The oldest became marquis after Grandpapa and had one son. He died, and his son Jared inherited the title. Of the three middle sons, the one who went into the church never married, and the other two had only daughters. Papa was the youngest, and he had Kit, so Kit is our cousin Jared's heir.''

"But only if this Jared doesn't produce a son,'' Esme objected.

"Oh, but he has never married, and now he's quite old,'' Constance said. "Almost as old as Uncle Frederick, I should think.''

"Well, nearly five-and-thirty, at any rate,'' Dru amended.

"That is scarcely too old to father a son,'' Esme said practically.

"But no decent girl would marry him,'' Dru said. "And though he is deep in degradation, I think he can never be quite dead to all feeling of what he owes his name. He would never *marry* one of his—his lightskirts.''

"Degradation? Is he really so bad then?''

"He has made a career out of embarrassing the family,'' Dru said. "You can imagine how our uncle the archbishop feels. Jared began when he was only one-and-twenty. He wanted to marry a lady whose father had quarrelled with Grandpapa and forbade the banns. He tried to run off with her; her brother followed, and they fought a duel. They thought the brother would not survive, and Jared was obliged to flee the country."

"And has he been pining for her all these years then?" Esme wanted to know.

"I shouldn't think so," Hope said. "She married someone else and has six children and has grown quite stout."

"No, he has simply been racketing around the Continent, getting embroiled in one scandal after another. It is said there is scarcely a high-flier in all of Europe who has not lived under his protection at one time or another. And he frequents every gaming hell."

"But how do you know that?"

"Why, everyone who goes abroad has seen him in one of those haunts."

"But if they frequent those haunts, why should they condemn him for doing the same?"

"It is quite different to visit one of those places as a tourist curiosity," Dru said, very much on her dignity, "but *he* seems quite at home there."

"Has he lost the family fortune?"

"No, he seems inordinately lucky." Dru bit her lip. "But that doesn't make it any better."

"Not better perhaps, but more comfortable," Esme said wisely, having had some experience in such matters.

"And then he was involved in some raffish adventure, running a French blockade to take supplies to a besieged city."

"That sounds very commendable," Esme commented.

"Yes, only afterward he declared he'd only done it because his current mistress's brother was one of the besieged, and it was the only way to coax a kiss from her."

"And you see what makes it all the worse," Hope added, "is that he has come back to England several times *flaunting* one of these dashers on his arm. That really will not do, you know. Mamas of any decent girl positively flee from the sight of him. No, he will never marry now, even if he should wish to, and one can hardly suppose he does at his age."

Privately, Esme thought her cousins were rather naive about the fleeing mamas. Some might flee in horror, true, but when the day came that a wealthy marquis of five-and-thirty couldn't find *some* well-born wife to wed, if he should put his mind to it, monkeys would fly. But if he were as far sunk in iniquity as they said, perhaps indeed he was not looking for a wife.

"Well then," she said, "if it's the title Lydia wants and there's no way to avoid Kit's inheriting it, then he must just stiffen his resolve and refuse to offer for her. They aren't betrothed, are they?"

"No, it's understood that he will establish himself first so that he can take her to Tydings to live, for though I'm sure our cousin Jared lives a reckless and imprudent life—drinking and so on—still, if he isn't killed in a duel, he may linger for years. But it's no good to talk of Kit stiffening his resolve. This is the only thing Uncle Frederick has ever asked of him. How *can* he say no? Heaven knows what would have become of Mama and the rest of us when Papa died if Uncle Frederick hadn't given us a home."

"It hasn't been all one-sided," Esme said. "Your mama runs his household for him with every consideration for his comfort. And all of you give him the pleasantest of companionship. *Per mi aviso*—in my opinion, to think that Kit must *repay* him by marrying a woman he doesn't care for is barbaric."

Dru wrung her hands. "Oh Esme, you don't understand. Uncle Frederick would never say such a thing as that Kit had to repay him. But he believes so strongly in duty and has always drummed it into our heads. Kit has known for years that it was expected of him, and if he should refuse, Mama would be so hurt. I vow she would hardly think she could stay on living here so comfortably if Kit refused to offer for Lydia."

"I think Esme is right," Constance declared. "It *is* barbaric. Kit should run away with Verena!"

"Connie, never say such a thing!" her elder sister cried. "Would you want Kit to turn out like the wicked marquis? Why, the Gaylords are such a very proper family—they would never receive Verena again if she eloped, and she is so devoted to all of them it would break her heart."

For a moment, Esme had caught a glimmer of hope in Constance's suggestion, but she recognised that an elopement would put the lovers beyond the pale in many circles. "We'll just have to put our minds to it and think of something else then," she decided.

"It's useless to hope," Dru said, "for it isn't only Uncle Frederick who is pushing the match. Cousin Jared says he must offer for her too, and if Kit doesn't obey, Jared could make it very hard for him. As Kit is his heir, Jared paid his Oxford fees and he makes him an allowance."

"The wicked marquis? And why should he wish for Kit to marry Lydia?" Esme wanted to know.

The girls looked embarrassed. Then Dru said, "Oh, it's all because of a youthful peccadillo of Kit's. When he was quite young, he developed a foolish *tendre* for a dashing widow who resided briefly in the district. He wrote her some letters and—well, Uncle Frederick appealed to Jared to intervene. Jared bought the woman off, but lately Uncle Frederick wrote to Jared again and told him Kit was showing reluctance to make a formal offer for a girl of excellent background, though both their families had favoured the match for years, and that he feared Kit was likely to get into more trouble as he had before, so Jared wrote and told Kit that he was to offer for Lydia or no one else, and he wanted to hear nothing more of such scrapes as the widow."

"Which is terribly unfair coming from someone of his history," Hope said indignantly.

"Well, it doesn't seem to me that it was very handsome of Uncle Frederick either," Esme said.

"No, but that doesn't mend the problem."

"Cheer up, cousins. We'll think of something," Esme promised, but by their doubtful looks she could see they didn't put much faith in the notion.

"Truly we will," she added, hating to see them all so sunk in gloom.

"I don't see what's to be thought of," Hope said.

"Well, of course you don't," Esme replied. "If you had, you'd already have done it. But it's not at all to the point to sit around in a hen-hearted way, wringing our hands and wishing things were different."

"I should not say we are hen-hearted!" Dru took violent exception to her cousin's remark. "In fact," she tossed her head, "we have already thought up several plans and . . . it is only that they would make things worse than before."

"That would seem to be a drawback," Esme commented wryly. "What were these plans?"

"Well," Dru offered reluctantly, "we thought that if Kit fell into disgrace, then Lydia wouldn't want to marry him, only it would have to be something quite terrible to make her give up wishing to be a marchioness—something like treason or murder."

Esme stared at Dru in amazement. "I would be the first to agree that Lydia Milliman is not *dolce*, but I should think that even a bad marriage would be preferable for Kit to death on the gallows."

"I told you we had rejected the plan," Dru said defensively. "And just a small disgrace probably would not serve, because it would very likely not turn Lydia away, and poor Kit would be left with the bad character, and Mama would feel it too keenly even to contemplate."

"If only Papa were alive," Esme mused, "he could think of something, I daresay. That is, if Mama were alive too, because after losing her, he was not at all good at thinking up plans. But in the old days—why the opera was as full of plots behind the scenes as on the stage. I remember once when

35

Signora Rindoni was piqued over not getting a rise in her salary and pretended she had lost her voice. She was really a great coloratura, and Papa did not at all want to sing that night with a rather trifling substitute they had brought in, so he set one of Signora Rindoni's costumes ablaze right in the middle of her dressing room, and she was obliged to scream, 'Fire! Fire!'—only in Italian, of course—loud enough for them to hear her in Turin. Papa vowed it was a miracle that her voice was restored to her, and of course there was nothing for her to do but go on and sing that night.''

"But what about the fire?'' Constance wanted to know, her eyes wide.

"Oh, Papa had buckets of water handy and doused the flames. He always said you should never set a blaze unless you were sure you could quench it.''

"I don't see how setting Lydia's clothes on fire would solve anything,'' Connie said.

"Of course not, goosecap. I never suggested it would. I only said Papa was good at thinking up plans.''

"Maybe we could give her poison and withhold the antidote until she promised to renounce Kit,'' Hope suggested.

Esme shot her a half-admiring glance for the spirit of the suggestion, if not for its practicality. "Do you know any poisons with certain antidotes?'' she asked. "And if you did, do you think she would stick to her word once she had been given it?''

"No, it's quite hopeless,'' Dru said glumly. "The only thing that will save Kit is if Mama comes unexpectedly into a great fortune so that she needn't feel beholden to Uncle Frederick, or if Mr. Milliman loses all his money and land, but I shouldn't think that likely because Mr. Milliman is a most prudent man and never goes near the gaming tables.''

"Well then, is there anyone who might leave your mama a fortune?''

"I can't imagine who. There were only the four of them, you know; Mama and your mama, and Uncle Frederick and their younger brother, our Uncle Phillip. But Phillip is not at all wealthy, having only a modest place in Sussex and five children besides. His eldest son is Uncle Frederick's heir unless, of course, my uncle should remarry and have a son.''

"How about eccentric rich aunts? One hears often about their bestowing largesse in the very nick of time,'' Esme said.

Dru shook her head. "I'm afraid there was only one with any property—a great-aunt on Mama's side, and though she was very well to pass, she was scarcely wealthy, and what she had she left to Phillip. And the Channing aunts all have children of their own.''

"Poor Kit is doomed,'' Hope said in tragic accents.

"Nonsense,'' Esme said bracingly. "We shall contrive something—just see if we don't. Lydia Milliman must certainly not have Kit. I shall put my mind to it, and some way we will come up with a plan to save him.''

4

IT WAS NOT many days later when Drusilla went to Esme's bedchamber just as her cousin was putting the final touches to her riding costume. "Do you think this is the proper angle for these coq feathers, Dru?" She peered critically into the mirror.

"Oh yes, they do nicely," Dru said impatiently, "but only guess what exciting news I have. Well, you couldn't of course, so I will tell you. Sir Aldwin Grey is giving a ball—a real ball, mind, not a rout party like the Millimans'—and we are both invited!"

Esme pulled the feathers a little forward so that they curled around her cheek. "Well, that sounds very pleasant. We are becoming gay to dissipation."

"Oh, do stop fiddling with those feathers and come along," Dru said, pulling her cousin by the arm as they started for the stables to begin their morning ride. "I don't think you perfectly understand. This will be an affair of the first stare of elegance. Sir Aldwin lives some distance away, so we do not often meet him, but he is perhaps the most important man in the district."

"Is he married?" Esme wanted to know.

Dru glanced at her sharply, ready to dampen any pretensions her cousin might have along the line of attracting the notice of such a man. "No, he is not. Why do you ask?"

"I was just thinking. If he's so important, maybe he would do for Lydia."

Dru stared. "What can you mean—for Lydia?"

Esme didn't answer as the groom was just leading her pretty Peaseblossom out. In fact, she did not speak until they were well away into the south meadow.

"What I meant was, if Sir Aldwin is so important, perhaps Lydia can be persuaded to have him instead of Kit."

Dru burst out laughing. "What Kit would say is that you're queer in your attic, Cousin!"

"But surely you see," Esme said patiently, "all that talk of poisoning Lydia was just nonsense. We must be practical, and the *most* practical thing would be if she chose someone else. Then the burden of blame wouldn't lie with Kit, and he wouldn't have to undergo spasms of guilt regarding his mama and Uncle Frederick."

"Well, when it comes to Sir Aldwin, you're fair and far out. He and the Millimans aren't even on close terms. They meet cordially because not to do so would cause talk, but there is no love lost between them—some quarrel years ago between Mr. Milliman and Sir Aldwin's father, I believe."

"Mmmm," Esme mused. "Like Romeo and Juliet. That might be an advantage."

Dru went into whoops. "*No* one but you could see Lydia and Sir Aldwin as a pair of star-crossed lovers. They are both far too sensible to behave like a *drama*."

"She would be entitled to call herself Lady."

"But her aunt married a baron. A baronet wouldn't satisfy Lydia's ambitions at all, even if Sir Aldwin could be brought to the point. No, Esme, you must disabuse yourself of the notion that Lydia will substitute Sir Aldwin for Kit."

Disappointed but not totally cast down, Esme said, "However, in principle, it is a very good notion. Somewhere we must find someone she *would* take in Kit's place." They rode on in silence for a few minutes. Then she brightened. "If it's the title she's mad for, then wouldn't it be quicker if she married the wicked marquis directly? She could save years of waiting for him to die and Kit to inherit."

Dru gave a little scream. "You are definitely touched in the upper works, Cousin!" she said inelegantly when she could speak. "Of all the absurdities. If you knew the prime articles of virtue that catch Locklynde's eye, you would know he would never give Lydia a glance, even if he were here where he *could* glance at her, which he isn't. But you have met Lydia, and how you can believe she would take a dissolute, depraved man of five-and-thirty when she can have Kit for the lift of a finger—"

"Well, she can't," Esme said flatly. "She can lift her finger all she wants, but we'll have to find a way to stop her from having Kit. It's too odious to contemplate."

Dru's face was very sober. "Yes, it is odious. All the same, you must get it through your mind that there's nothing you can do."

Esme's jaw tightened. "We'll see about that," she said and, giving Peaseblossom a sharp tap with her quirt, went galloping across the meadow.

Contriving a suitable gown for the ball took a great deal of Esme's attention during the next days, for she had nothing fine enough in her wardrobe; but, to her cousins' admiration, she transformed a plain green silk dress by adding an overskirt of white tulle and a rouleau of tulle at the décolletage, twisted with narrow gold braid from her box of bits and pieces. With a gold reticule that had been her mama's and a pair of gold silk roses to tuck into her dark curls, they declared she would take the shine out of half the ladies there.

Kit's mood had lightened perceptibly in the days since the Millimans' rout, and Esme felt more determined than ever that all his charm and good nature must not be wasted on Lydia, nor indeed on any lady who had not captured his whole heart.

The drive to Sir Aldwin Grey's estate took the better part of an hour, and the rooms were already crowded when the party from Wellspring House arrived. Upon being presented to her host, a stolid gentleman of some thirty years with prominent blue eyes and a humourless mouth, Esme thought he might do very well for Lydia.

The Millimans were not yet among the guests, so Kit asked Esme to stand up with him for the first set. He led her out on the floor in a lighthearted way. By the time their dance had ended, Esme caught sight of Lydia and her mother entering the ballroom. Mrs. Milliman beckoned to Kit in a peremptory way to which he responded with tight-lipped resignation.

Esme took the opportunity to explore the other rooms where guests were wandering about and decided that whatever the reason was for Sir Aldwin's importance, it could not be that he was an art collector, for all the pictures were extremely bad except for one Canaletto view of Venice, which was hanging in a dim passageway where it could scarcely be seen.

She was invited to join several sets by personable young gentlemen whom she had met previously, and eventually Sir Aldwin himself was kind enough to ask her to stand up with him, a condescension which Lady Channing seemed to find astonishingly good-natured of him.

He was rather silent at first, which she ascribed to his needing to mind his steps, but after some time it was apparent that even with utmost concentration he had difficulty keeping to the beat, so she ventured a little conversation. She complimented him on the success of his ball and told him it was the first she had attended since arriving in England.

"I do think it is going well," he replied gravely. "I daresay it is not quite what you are used to in foreign parts. In my house we do not waltz, for instance. My physician has assured me it is very bad for the liver."

"The l-liver?" Esme echoed faintly.

"All that twirling around makes one bilious," he assured her. "I recommend that you refrain, should the opportunity arise at some future date for you to take part in waltzing."

"I will certainly remember that," she said, thinking that

Dru was correct in believing that Sir Aldwin and Lydia were miscast as a pair of star-crossed lovers. However, if one left out the star-crossed part, it did seem to her that they were well suited to each other.

"I have had the pleasure of meeting some of your guests previously," she told him. "The Millimans, in fact, are close neighbours of ours. Miss Milliman is such a talented young lady and so decorously behaved."

Sir Aldwin made no response to this lure, so Esme said, "To think that such an attractive girl will someday have the responsibility of all her father's acres! It has some very pretty farmland."

"But I believe the number of trout in his stream is very small. And his coverts have little to recommend them," he said depressingly.

"What do you raise on your estate, Sir Aldwin?" she inquired.

"I have some of the best quail- and pheasant-shooting in the county. If I told you the extent of some of the enormous bags made here last year at my shooting parties, it would make you stare." And he went on to recount the numbers of birds slaughtered on various weekend shoots until, though she was not precisely staring, her eyes did indeed begin to glaze over.

She tried to introduce the topics of crops and cattle, but he seemed unconcerned with what his land was producing other than game. By the time he had recounted the weights of the largest trout taken from his stream in each of the last several years, she thought a change of topic was in order and asked what he thought of the tax bill presently up before the House.

He frowned. "I always leave that sort of thing to the members. That's what they're there for, don't you agree?"

She was not altogether sorry when the dance ended, but she was more convinced than ever that Sir Aldwin and Lydia deserved each other.

When she had the opportunity, she approached Lydia,

who was standing on the sidelines, fanning herself with the air of one who has been too busy dancing all the evening to take a breath of air. "It is a pleasant ball, is it not?" Esme asked. "Sir Aldwin's house is so large and elegant—quite a mansion, really."

"I daresay it would seem so to you," Lydia answered.

Cat, Esme thought, but persevered. "And his lands are quite extensive too, are they not? My aunt told me that his mother, Lady Grey, died several years ago. Such a shame. This great place really cries out for a hostess."

"Perhaps you think you could give it the touch it needs," Lydia said acidly.

"Oh, hardly," Esme returned. "I am sure Sir Aldwin deserves an heiress at the least and someone whose position in the county is securely established."

"Perhaps, though an heiress of good family might be forgiven for looking higher than a baronet."

Esme gave it up in disgust. There seemed to be no way to kindle a spark of interest between these two. She still thought the *idea* was sound, though. The trouble was that Sir Aldwin appeared not to be attractive enough to lure Lydia away from Kit, nor did she have anything of interest to offer Sir Aldwin. She devoted the remainder of the evening to making herself pleasant to her new acquaintances.

After the long carriage ride home, and when she was undressed and in her night robe, she went to Dru's room to brush her hair while they had a gossip about the ball. "You must tell me," Esme declared, "for I am fair dying of curiosity—*what* is Sir Aldwin's secret?"

Drusilla was bewildered. "Why, what can you mean? What secret should he have?"

"You told me he was the most important man in the neighbourhood," Esme said, "but even after the most adroit questioning, I could not divine the secret of his greatness."

Drusilla gasped. "Esme, you were never pestering Sir Aldwin with *questions* as if he were some common person?"

"Certainly not, for you had told me he was most *un-*

common. I was supremely tactful, but he was so reticent I could discover nothing. Tell me," her eyes were sparkling, "did he perform some heroic feat—save the king's life, perhaps, or that of one of the royal dukes?"

"Why, Esme Leonardo! What strange twists your mind takes! Why should you imagine such a thing?"

"Well, I knew right off that he could not be an artist or musician, and he didn't show any interest in politics. I thought maybe he had made some marvellous new improvements in agriculture, but he hardly seemed to know what crops were grown on his acres. So you must tell me, Dru, where *is* it that Sir Aldwin's talents lie?"

"I'm sure I don't know what you mean. Sir Aldwin is the richest man in the neighbourhood."

"A great financier, you mean?" Esme asked doubtfully.

"No, of course not. He is just very rich. His holdings are the largest and his house the finest and his income the greatest of anyone around."

"But what does he *do*?" Esme was clearly puzzled. "He must have some talents."

"Kit says his coats are made by Weston and that he can tie his neckcloth in the finest Mathematical he has ever seen."

Esme burst into laughter. "Oh, you are roasting me. Nobody could be such a goose as to believe tying a neckcloth is important. Give over now and tell me Sir Aldwin's secret."

"He is very rich," Drusilla said stiffly. "He has no secret."

"But inherited riches—why, that's only an accident of birth. It doesn't make one important," she objected.

"I daresay you have led a very different sort of life," Drusilla said with a set to her lips, "but if you wish to fit into life in the country, you will have to understand that not everyone is a famous opera singer or anything of that nature, and that people are looked up to for quite different reasons."

"But—" Esme began, and then at her cousin's implacable

look she saw that she had offended, and she stopped. "Well, yes, I'm sure I want to learn to fit in," and turning the subject, inquired, "Tell me, didn't you think Lady Wescott's dress the most delicious confection?"

By the time the two were ready for their beds, Esme thought that she had been half-forgiven, but only half.

Within a very few days, the slight coolness between the girls was forgotten. One morning Esme, Hope, and Constance were in the morning room perusing a fashion periodical, arguing over the merits of an ermine tippet as against one of sable, when Dru came dashing into the room, her honey-coloured curls tumbling in such a dishevelled way about her ears that for a startled moment Esme feared some dire emergency had discommoded her cousin, but a look at her shining eyes dispelled that notion.

"Oh, it is all settled! Mama has just told me that we are all to go up to London. Uncle Frederick has hired a most unexceptionable house in Hanover Square—only fancy! And Esme and I are both to make our come-outs this Season."

"How glad you must be that Esme came to us, Dru," Hope exclaimed, "for I know you feared you would have to wait until I was old enough so that he could fire both of us off into the *ton* at once for economy's sake. I only hope I won't have to wait for Connie, but if either of you manages to land a really plump catch, I shall expect you to do something quite handsome for both of us."

"Hope!" her elder sister said, shocked. "This talk of 'plump catches' is most unbecoming, and nothing could exceed my uncle's generosity. We are to have dress allowances as well as use of the carriage, and while he is taking most of the servants from Wellspring House up with us, he has hired two extra footmen and a maid."

"Indeed, that is generous," Esme said, though she could not help being struck by Hope's suggestion that getting two girls off for the price of one was indeed an economy.

All fanciful notions of ermine and sable tippets were

dispelled now as the girls settled down to serious discussions of what new clothes could actually be afforded. Of course, for really important ball gowns, a London modiste was almost de rigueur, Lady Channing said, but as costs in town were bound to be dearer, she vowed that Miss Pynchon in the village could help stretch their budget by providing morning dresses, carriage dresses, walking dresses, and so on that would look very smart as her skill was by no means to be despised.

Of course, it was to be expected that Drusilla would have the more extensive wardrobe, for while their uncle had placed an equal sum at each girl's disposal, Dru's mama could contribute her mite, too. However, with very real sacrifice she made a sincere offer to divide the amount she could afford between the two, but Esme would not hear of it.

"No, no ma'am, I shall do very well. You will see. I am quite good at contriving, and I can make any number of my own things, which will save the cost of a dressmaker, and I have lashings of lace and other trimmings that will be a real saving, too. Besides, it would be false economy if Dru were not to appear at her very best for you know she is so beautiful that she is much more likely to go off than I. Indeed, with my lack of fortune I cannot really hope to make a match at all, and certainly not a distinguished one, but I shall enjoy a social Season very much all the same. However, what with the Channing nose and being granddaughter to a marquis, Dru has every hope of something splendid, so our best efforts should be concentrated on her."

Lady Channing's eyes misted over. "What a good girl you are, Esme," she said, choking slightly.

Esme's most pressing need was for a new riding habit, as even *her* optimistic nature could not convince her that her shabby green one, though adequate for the country, would serve in London, and Uncle Frederick had allowed that the girls might take their mounts to the city. Indeed, to be seen riding in Hyde Park was very nearly a prerequisite for any girl of social ambitions.

Though the cost cut alarmingly into her budget, she at last settled upon a habit of claret kerseymere with a matching rakish hat that sat most dashingly upon her dark curls.

The time until their departure passed almost too quickly between poring over patterns in fashion magazines, shopping trips for muslins, and fittings at Miss Pynchon's. Lady Channing declared that Esme would be worn to a frazzle before she ever reached town if she did not leave off her incessant stitching, but Esme was determined to save as much as she could on her dresses so that the sum she had left for slippers, gloves, and a ball gown or two might not prove too meagre even for one of her economical habits.

The remove to London was not accomplished without a good deal of fuss and botheration, but after days of orders and counter-orders to the servants, and packing and re-packing, they eventually found themselves settled into the house in Hanover Square which, while not absolutely splendid, was well enough and could scarcely be despised by any but the most finicking. The kitchens were not as well equipped as Lady Channing would have liked, and the library was a bit cramped, but the entrance hall was graceful, the double staircase all that could be desired, and the dining hall almost lavish in size.

One of their first callers was Verena Gaylord. She embraced Dru and the younger girls and then held out her hand to Esme. "How fortunate your cousins are to have such a delightful addition to their family," she said. "Drusilla and I correspond, you know, and she has told me so much about you."

Esme surveyed the girl who her cousins had told her was Kit's choice. She was of medium height and very slender. Her burnished brown hair had golden lights, and her eyes were halfway between grey and green. Her features were delicate in her heart-shaped face, but it was her expression of sweetness that struck one first.

Esme took her hand in a firm grasp. Yes, she thought, Verena would do very well for Kit. He came into the room just then and, at the sight of the hungry flash of yearning in his face when he saw Verena, Esme found a lump in her throat and almost had to turn away.

Verena's eyelids came down and hid her expression just for a moment as he bent over her hand. Then she looked up and gave him a blindingly lovely smile.

Esme clenched her fists until her nails cut into her palms. If the Marquis of Locklynde could have seen the way those two looked at each other—just in that first unguarded moment—surely it would have melted even *his* stony heart. Though perhaps, if her cousins' reports were true, he didn't have a heart at all. Perhaps he could be run right through with a sword and not even bleed.

Verena had come to tell them that an invitation card would shortly arrive for a Venetian breakfast her mother was holding on Wednesday and that they must be sure to save the day. Lady Channing came into the room shortly and of course acquiesced to this plan, for the Gaylords were old friends. Though she could not like Kit's being thrown too much into Verena's company, they would be bound to meet everywhere, and she was confident that under the circumstances he would not go beyond the line.

Other callers arrived, and Verena took her leave. Kit continued to converse pleasantly with the new visitors for a little while before he found an excuse to retire from the drawing room, but his face had a bruised look that constricted his mama's heart.

5

WHILE HOPE AND Constance were too young for the social whirl, they were still able to enjoy the sights of London along with their older sister and cousin, and they were delighted by everything they saw. If Esme, having visited several of the capitals of Europe, was not quite so impressed as the Channing girls, still she found much to be pleased with. If St. Paul's seemed stark in design compared to the intricacies of the Cathedral of Milano, she never let such an heretical notion cross her lips; and if the Royal Academy struck her as the beginnings of a nice little collection of artwork but one that could as yet in no way compare with the museums of Florence, still the very Englishness of many of the paintings was refreshing to her eye.

She very much enjoyed Hyde Park, whether riding Peaseblossom in the morning, strolling with Dru, or being driven at the fashionable hour in Kit's curricle. On one such occasion, when Dru held the reins, they came opposite an extremely elegant high-perch phaeton in which the lady being driven was so striking that Esme could not help staring. She was very beautiful in a theatrical way, dressed in the latest style: all in black save for a white ostrich plume in her hat and a knot of white roses pinned at her throat. Esme tried to see the gentleman who was driving, but by now the black crown of the lady's hat obscured her companion's face, and all she could see were his smart caped driving coat and two strong hands expertly handling the reins of a spirited pair of chestnuts.

Dru gave a gasp and then flicked Kit's greys sharply to move on at a faster pace. Her lips were set in a disapproving line.

"Do you know that lady?" Esme asked, curious.

"No, I do not, and *lady* is hardly the word. That is Theodosia Wild, or so she calls herself. She was Cousin Locklynde's mistress, whom he brought back from heaven-knows-where the last time he graced these shores with his presence. He went away again and left her here—to do very well for herself, apparently. And now he is back, for that was he driving her, and what Mama will say I do not know!"

"Oh, why didn't you tell me sooner?" Esme wailed, turning to try to catch a glimpse of the infamous marquis, but only the back of his curly beaver hat and a pair of broad shoulders were visible as the phaeton disappeared around a bend in the path. She felt a keen disappointment at not seeing more closely the man about whom she had heard so much.

"He can't have been long in town, or we should have heard gossip," Dru said. "Thank Providence the day is not fine and there are so few people driving in the park. Oh, I hope he will take himself off again soon, down to Locklynde Hall or, better yet, out of England altogether."

"I wish I might meet him first. I should like to give him a raking down for the way he has interfered in Kit's life," Esme said stoutly.

Dru shuddered. "I doubt you would have the courage to do so. My cousin is a most formidable man. Oh, what a time for him to appear—just as we are making our come-outs and want to seem most respectable. Letting himself be seen in the park with Theodosia Wild! That expensive equipage they were driving in was a gift to her from him, I believe."

"He has good taste," Esme murmured.

"Taste!" Dru snapped. "To parade that barque of frailty before all London? Oh, it is all of a piece with his other endeavours to put the family to the blush. And she lives in a very pretty little house in Belgrave Square, right between the

Montgroves and the Bookertons. They are such high sticklers—I wonder how they like having her for a neighbour?"

"How did you happen to meet her?" Esme wondered.

"Meet her! I would scarcely have *met* her. A year ago, Mama came up to London to attend the wedding of one of our cousins. She brought Kit and me with her. We stayed on for a few days and attended the theatre one night. My cousin, the marquis, was there in a box with that *creature* for all the world to stare at. When he saw Mama and Kit, for I don't suppose he even recognised me, he rose and gave us the most insolent bow. Mama was so humiliated we did not even stay for the rest of the play but slipped out at the next interval. You should have seen That Woman—wearing black as she was today, but her corsage cut so low it was indecent, and her throat blazing with diamonds. I heard our cousins talking about it the next day—that's how I found out her name—and then later in the park we saw them riding, and Jared raised his whip and saluted Mama as they passed by. She almost went into spasms, for our cousins said that not only was Miss Wild the most expensive sort of high-flier, but she was at one time suspected of having been a spy."

"Well, you can't believe every rumour of *that* sort," Esme said.

"Nevertheless, she is a most unsuitable person," Dru said primly.

Esme giggled. "Well, it could hardly be otherwise. One can scarcely be a high-flier and a suitable person too. It's a contradiction in terms."

Dru gave her cousin a glance of reproach. "Sometimes your levity goes beyond the line, Esme. You must have a care not to be thought too continental in your outlook."

Meekly, Esme subsided. "I'll try," she promised, but there was a gleam of amusement in her eyes.

To Drusilla's and Lady Channing's infinite relief, nothing more was heard of the marquis as the days passed, though

Esme felt a secret disappointment when he did not present himself in their drawing room, for not only did she have a lively curiosity to see what so depraved a man might look like, but she also had visions of herself daring to stand up to him to present Kit's case. Dru might think her courage would fail her at such an undertaking, but Esme felt that in the circumstances she could be a tigress.

She had no chance to prove her valour, however ". . . for he must have left town," her aunt said thankfully. "One cannot imagine Locklynde on the scene without scandal-broth brewing, and I have not heard a word about him from a soul save Lucia Finchley, who told me all agog that her son Josiah fancied he had seen him in the park, and though it put me into a quake, I assured her we had heard nothing from him and reminded her how short sighted Josiah is and so passed it off very well, I think. Oh, I pray that wherever he has taken himself off to, he will *stay*."

As Esme had predicted, Drusilla was an instant success at their very first party and never lacked for partners. She was looking ethereal in palest blue, and her manners, which were not so retiring as to make her tongue-tied or coy, were modest enough that she showed just the blend of shyness and charm that was bound to please. Esme recognised an absolutely smitten look in at least three pairs of masculine eyes as their owners gazed upon Dru's fair loveliness.

Somewhat to her surprise, Esme herself could not be classed as a wallflower either, though the men who seemed attracted to her were of a very different sort than Dru's beaux, more inclined to laugh with her than to languish over her. The most attractive of them was Captain James Kendall, and his smile was so infectious that Esme wondered whether, with a little effort, she might be able to become smitten with him.

Their first days of gaiety were bound to be especially enjoyable, for the Millimans had not yet come up to London, and therefore they were not meeting Lydia everywhere. Kit was able to stand up for two dances with Verena at every party without the consciousness of being watched by Lydia's possessive eyes, though of course his manners were far too good for him to make a parade of his feelings, and no one could have accused him of dangling after Verena or living in her pocket.

One night when Esme had gone to Dru's bedchamber to have a gossip about the party they had just attended, she said thoughtfully, "I suppose Verena knows about the pressure being put on Kit to offer for Lydia."

"Yes, I believe so. It is very sad to see how well-suited they are and yet how hopeless it is."

Esme frowned. "Nothing is hopeless till the knot is tied. And if Verena thought it were hopeless, wouldn't she avoid Kit?"

"Well, I suppose when one is in love, one clutches at straws," Dru said. "Perhaps she thinks something yet may happen."

"Such as?" Esme prompted.

"Oh, that Uncle Frederick will relent. Or—or—" here she hesitated—"suppose something should happen to Locklynde? If Kit were to become marquis *soon*, he would be rich enough that he wouldn't have to feel guilty about disobliging Uncle Frederick. He could make it up to him in a hundred different ways and set Mama up in style, too."

"I hope Verena is not placing her reliance on a happening that seems so unlikely," Esme said. "Dissolute or not, five-and-thirty is no great age, and the wicked marquis does not sound to me like the kind of man to stick his spoon in the wall for the convenience of his family."

Perhaps the handsomest man they had met in London was Mr. Sidney Porterfield, who held a minor post with the exchequer and had served abroad in the army during the war. He was several inches above six feet tall, with fine blue eyes set below a nobly proportioned forehead. His dark hair had just the right degree of curl to look well in a Stanhope crop, and his broad shoulders in the well-cut coats he wore obviously owed nothing to buckram wadding.

He seemed to be received everywhere and was the darling of hostesses, despite his lack of fortune, because his good looks and polished manners made him an embellishment at any social gathering.

One day while Dru was busy with a fitting for a new gown, Esme went with Verena and two other girls whose acquaintance she had made to the Pantheon Bazaar to purchase a few trifles. When she arrived home, she found Dru had returned and was with her sisters in the morning room.

"I'm glad to find you here," Esme cried, "for I heard something today which might be very useful. You know I went shopping with Verena and the Misses Curtiss and in the carriage on the way home, they fell to gossiping about Mr. Porterfield."

Dru gazed at her, an arrested look in her blue eyes.

"As you know, he hasn't a fortune of his own, and of course money is always useful to grease the wheels if one is making a career in the government."

"That's scarcely news," Hope said.

"No, but only listen. Did you know he was the younger son of a baron—the *much* younger son, with only sisters between him and his older brother? His brother has the barony now but is said to be quite frail, as well as having a wife who is past forty. And they have only daughters!"

"Well, of what use is that to *us*?" Constance demanded.

"Why, that it is almost a surety that Mr. Porterfield will eventually become a baron, but that day may be some way off, and I believe it is not really a great estate, so it would be well for him to marry money. And if Lydia were a baroness, it would make her equal to her aunt."

"Esme, are you proposing some intrigue that will bring Lydia and Mr. Porterfield together?" Hope cried. "That is fanciful beyond reason."

"It is certainly worth a try if it would bring your brother and Verena happiness," Esme retorted. "*Non e vero?*"

"Well, I think it's horrible," Dru burst out, "—scheming to entrap poor Mr. Porterfield with a girl like Lydia!"

"Better him than Kit," Esme said calmly, "because Kit is entrapped by his sense of duty to his uncle and your mama. If Mr. Porterfield allows himself to be trapped, it will be by his own greed."

"How beastly you are," Dru cried, "playing with people's lives as if they mattered no more than a set of chess pieces!"

"Well, isn't that what Uncle Frederick and Mr. Milliman have done—tried to move Kit and Lydia around as if they were pawns? You were not averse before to my trying to think of a plan, but now your defense of Mr. Porterfield would almost lead one to think that you—" She broke off, and one startled glance at Dru's heaving bosom and flaming cheeks told her more than she wished to know. So that was the way the wind was blowing!

"Oh, well, I daresay it was an idiotish thought," she said quickly and opened her parcels to distract the younger girls. "What do you think of this parasol, Hope? Will it not look charmingly with my primrose walking dress?"

At the Penroses' ball, Esme was pleased to meet Lady Dartney again, she who had been so very kind to her when she had first arrived at the Channings' and had said such heartwarming things about Esme's mama.

"Come here, child, and let me look at you," Lady Dartney exclaimed. "I declare you have the same sense of style about you as your mama had. Of course the clothes we wore then would seem stiff and fusty to you now, but your mama always knew what became her—just as you do."

Esme flushed with pleasure. She was wearing a gown of silk in an apricot shade, quite simple but excellently cut. Lady Dartney took her hand. "Let me present you to Lady Tilton. Maria, this is Estella Hasborough's daughter. Come and sit by us for a few minutes and tell Lady Tilton your adventures, Esme. She was a great friend of your mama, too."

Esme gladly did as she was bid, chatting easily with the

two ladies and answering all their questions until she saw Lady Dartney give a little shiver. "Oh ma'am, are you feeling cold? May I fetch your shawl for you?"

"Yes, I believe I would be more comfortable with it," the older woman said, and directed Esme where it might be found. When Esme returned with the shawl, she found her friend so deep in conversation with Lady Tilton that she forbore to interrupt but quietly took a seat beside the two until they were finished with their gossip.

"Good heavens, isn't that young Wittimore?" Lady Tilton was exclaiming. "Where do you suppose he found the ready to rig himself up for a Season? That's not an ill-fitting coat by any means."

"Well, it can mean only that things are in such desperate straits that he must find a wife," Lady Dartney said. "He's never been in the petticoat line, but I know for a fact that the old viscount left the estate in the shabbiest way when he died. Between his gaming and his disastrous foreign investments, I suppose the boy has found himself at *point non plus*. Perhaps he sold off a few last pictures or some unentailed acres to frank his Season in town. I'm sure there couldn't be much else left to sell. The place was falling to rack last time I was in the neighbourhood."

"Such a misfortune. It was a noble old house once," Lady Tilton said. "I've seen pictures of it in the guidebooks."

"Yes, but the decay set in before young Wittimore's father's time. He had to marry an heiress, too, though precious little good it did for the estate. Well, perhaps the boy will be more prudent—*if* he manages to marry money. I'd certainly hate to risk a daughter of mine on a Wittimore."

"Still," Lady Tilton said, "it's a very *old* title and the boy is well-enough looking."

"Yes. I knew his mama slightly, and she was a sweet girl, so I wish him luck. I won't let it pass my lips that he's desperate for a fortune. Perhaps he'll be able to carry the thing through, and if he does, perhaps he'll be a better manager than his father."

At this point Lady Dartney noticed her young friend waiting patiently by, and Esme stood up to slip the shawl around her shoulders. She asked if either of the ladies would like something to drink, and at that moment the young man in question strolled by. His eye seemed caught by Esme and then, upon recognising old acquaintance, came up to the two ladies and made a graceful bow. "Lady Tilton, Lady Dartney. It has been a long time since we met. I'm St. John Wittimore."

"Yes, of course. I remember you," Lady Dartney said. "Allow me to introduce you to my young friend, Miss Leonardo. Esme, this is the Viscount Wittimore."

"Do you dance this evening, Miss Leonardo?" the viscount inquired. "I believe a set is just forming."

"Why, thank you," Esme said, laying her hand on his arm and allowing him to lead her toward the dance floor. It occurred to her that Lady Dartney had not hesitated at introducing her to Wittimore, knowing that, almost penniless as she was, she stood in no danger from him.

"I have not seen you at any of the balls this Season, my lord," Esme said. "Are you just up to London?"

"Yes, I fear that the cares of running my estate leave me less time for pleasure than I could wish. My father died not so many months ago, and one hardly likes to leave a place like Gurnstone completely in the hands of one's agent."

"Gurnstone," Esme meditated, her eyes twinkling with amusement at his pretension. "I believe I have heard that name. Perhaps it appears in a guidebook."

"Yes," he sighed. "It is somewhat of a responsibility having such an historical place on one's hands. But now let us talk about you. I think I can guess the facts. You are having your first London Season and have bedazzled all who have set eyes on you."

"Why should you think that?" she asked.

"If it were not your first Season, you would not be *Miss* Leonardo, and you must bedazzle all beholders because you are surely the most elegant-looking creature on the floor."

The blatant flattery disgusted her a little, but suddenly a thought stunning in its implications came into her mind. The problem of working out an intricate plan distracted her almost to the point of her faltering in her execution of the steps of the dance. Then she gave a gay little laugh. "What a charming compliment, Lord Wittimore, especially so as I made this gown myself. You see, I am a pensioner of my uncle, who is giving me this Season, along with my cousin, and I do not like to put him to too much expense."

A blank look had come into his eyes and, though his lip did not quite curl in contempt, his smile was now quite forced.

"That is my cousin over there, the very beautiful girl in blue with the roses in her hair." She followed the hopeful cast of his glance and then, crushing his expectations, said, "She has cause to be grateful to our uncle, too, because, like mine, her father is dead, and though her circumstances are not quite as straitened as mine, without my uncle's generosity we should neither of us have this Season."

She could see that he was now itching to be rid of anyone so completely useless to his cause, and she sighed and said, "It is so exciting for us to be up in London. We live in a very modest neighbourhood. In fact, the only really *handsome* house nearby belongs to the Millimans. Perhaps you are acquainted with the family?"

There was a faint prick of interest in his eyes. "Let me see, perhaps I knew a Milliman boy at school."

"Oh no," she said. "They have only one child, their daughter Lydia. She is having her first Season, too, though she is not here tonight. Her mother had some trifling indisposition, I believe, and Lydia has such devotion to duty that she would not leave her."

"How very commendable," he said.

"Oh yes, Lydia is in all things commendable. She is not like some of these flighty girls who think of nothing but the social whirl. So many heiresses think of nothing but to spend money on furbelows and gaiety, but Lydia has a more serious cast of mind. However, she is not at all high in the instep, in spite of her position. In fact, she has consented to attend a small rout party we are holding on Thursday."

"Indeed?"

She let him wait in suspense for several minutes before she said with forced timidity, "Perhaps—that is, if you could spare us an hour—perhaps you would care to come?"

Very off-hand, he said, "If it is at all possible, I would be charmed to look in."

Well pleased with herself, she furnished him with the address in Hanover Square.

All the way home in the carriage, Esme contained herself well enough that her Aunt Dora was unaware of any undercurrents, save that she did remark that Esme and Drusilla both had a special sparkle in their eyes which she hoped betokened a pleasurable evening.

"Oh yes, Aunt," Esme breathed, adding to herself, *but not for the same reasons.*

Dru, however, had apparently caught some hint of her cousin's suppressed excitement for she appeared at the door of her bedchamber almost immediately after the abigail had finished undressing her, and was closely followed by Hope and Constance.

The girls piled onto Esme's bed, and Dru demanded, "Tell us, Esme. You're about to boil over with news."

"Has it to do with a man?" Hope asked. "You met someone marvellous?"

"A paragon," Esme assured her with a joyous little laugh. "*Just* what I've been looking for. I've invited him to our rout party."

"Oh, do tell us quickly," Constance begged. "Is he handsome? Is he tall? Did he fall instantly in love with you?"

Esme held up a protesting hand. "Don't rush me. Yes, his looks are well enough, and he is tall, and I think he fell in love with me instantly because I looked so *elegant*."

"Ohh," Hope breathed. "How exciting! And you did look elegant, Esme. You have such style."

"However," Esme continued, "he fell instantly *out* of love as soon as I confided my circumstances—that I am dependent upon Uncle Frederick and had made my own dress."

"Oh, Esme!" Dru cried, "surely not! You couldn't like a man who was so shabby."

"I tell you he's perfect," Esme insisted. "Hear me out. To begin with, he's a viscount. And it's a very *old* title. And he has an estate in Gloucestershire called Gurnstone, which is in the guidebooks."

"But Esme—" Dru began in puzzled dismay.

"You haven't heard the best part," Esme said, her eyes sparkling. She held them in suspense for another moment before she said, "His father was a wastrel; Gurnstone is crumbling to bits, and the viscount is hanging out for a rich wife to pull him out of the River Tick!"

Three pairs of eyes stared at her in blank astonishment. Finally Dru said, "You must be all about in the head."

"But don't you see—he's perfect. For Lydia!"

"For *Lydia*? Esme, you've run mad."

"I've already laid the foundation—that Lydia is an heiress and a serious-minded girl with an eye to duty, not some flibbertigibbet social butterfly. And I told him she'd be at our rout."

"Well, I can see if he's a fortune hunter that he might be interested in Lydia—"

"Yes, because at least her family is respectable," Esme interrupted. "It must be in his mind that he might have to sell his title to a wealthy cit's daughter."

"But why under heaven should Lydia be interested in *him*!"

"Well, for one thing because he'll be so interested in *her*.

That's one of the most powerful love potions known—having someone think you're wonderful. Unless, of course, you're an Incomparable who is so accustomed to adoration that it begins to pall. But that is surely not Lydia's case.''

"But she has her mind set on Kit. Why should she settle for some—some basket-scrambler?''

"I hope she won't find that out,'' Esme said. "Lady Dartney and Lady Tilton have agreed between them that they won't bruit it about, for his dead mother's sake. And he isn't well known in these parts. With any luck, he can keep his financial difficulties secret.''

"Esme Leonardo! You can't seriously believe Lydia would prefer him to Kit!'' Dru asked.

"Not right away. But if he makes himself agreeable enough, she might very well do so. After all, she can hardly have convinced herself that Kit is mad for love of her.''

"I shouldn't think Lydia's heart has much to do with it. And Kit is going to be a marquis. That's miles better than an impecunious viscount.''

"*Going* to be,'' Esme said. "That's what it all may hinge on. Would she rather be a viscountess now, or someday be a marchioness? *Meglio un uovo oggi che una gallina domani.* Better an egg today than a chicken tomorrow. As you said, the wicked marquis may linger for years while Lydia remains plain Mrs. Channing. And it can't have escaped her mind that it's not a dead certainty Kit will ever succeed to the title. Your cousin Jared could surprise you all by marrying and producing an heir who would cut Kit out.''

"Your plan will never work,'' Dru said.

"Very well, if you won't make the least push to keep that purse-mouthed crabster from becoming your sister-in-law, I shall have to do it all myself, for I'm persuaded that Kit's and Verena's happiness is worth the effort.''

"Well . . .'' Dru conceded at last, "I still think you have windmills where your brain should be, but I suppose it's worth a try.''

= 6 =

LADY CHANNING HAD settled on a rout party because, as she said, so early in the Season it might be considered too coming to hold a ball. She had been fortunate enough to obtain vouchers for both girls to Almack's, as well as a number of invitations of delightful variety, but one would not wish to push oneself forward by appearing to set oneself too high.

Also, her brother's purse was not quite so wide open as to run to balls as yet, and a fashionably crowded rout would prove a more effective social stroke than a ball which, as it was early days yet for both girls, might not be so well attended as to qualify as a shocking squeeze. But perhaps later, if something interesting enough were in the offing, Frederick might be persuaded to lay down his blunt for a full-fledged ball, she said, which words Esme interpreted to mean that if Dru had caught the eye of an important enough suitor, her uncle might be willing to show her off to advantage at her own ball if he believed it would aid in bringing her suitor up to scratch.

On the morning of the rout, their uncle presented to each girl a narrow gold bangle with such vociferous protestations that they must not thank him overmuch for these baubles—along with all else he was doing in their behalf —that they were both almost crushed under the burden of his oppressive generosity.

Their spirits began to rise, however, when it was time to dress for the party. Drusilla had chosen to wear white gauze over a pale pink silk underdress. The deep lace flounce at the bottom was caught up with tiny nosegays of roses and forget-me-nots. Two more of the nosegays held up her curls at each side of her face, and Esme thought the forget-me-nots were no bluer than her cousin's lovely eyes.

Esme was in white net over white crepe; the corsage above the high waist was of deep rose crepe, and the short sleeves were slashed with white satin ribbons. The hem was trimmed with a wide rouleau of white satin entwined with strands of pearl and interspersed with roses in the same shade as the corsage and sleeves. She had fashioned it herself, and it was something a little out of the ordinary style for a debutante, but she knew that her dark colouring was not flattered by pastels. The touches of deeper colour were by far more becoming to her complexion. Over her elbows she had placed a china crepe scarf in a matching rose shade embroidered in white, one of the treasures from her box, along with the pearl trimming for her dress.

Before they went down, Esme took Dru aside. "I think, Cousin, that it must be you who tells Lydia about the viscount. You must build him up as if he were a real prize. She has taken me in such dislike that if I talk about him, she would probably snub him to spite me, but you're Kit's sister and she would be bound to hear you out. You must emphasize the antiquity of the title and the magnificence of the pictures of Gurnstone that you've seen in the guidebooks. Do anything you can to pique her interest. He should be able to carry on from there if I read him rightly."

"Wild tales are more in your line, Cousin," Dru said with a glazed look, "but I shall do my best."

The house in Hanover Square looked exceedingly festive with baskets of cut flowers ranged about the rooms and all the chandeliers and girandoles aglitter with lighted candles.

As Esme had feared, Lydia and her mother were among the early arrivals, but Esme fiercely commanded Hope, who was being given the treat of appearing at the party, to draw

Lydia off into another room until after the viscount made his appearance.

Hope rose to the occasion nobly by saying, "Lydia, will you please come into the dining hall and give me your opinion on the seating arrangements?" Lydia's opinions were so well formed that she was always gratified to be able to share them, so she followed along without questioning why the seating arrangements should have been placed in Hope's hands.

Presently the viscount was announced and Esme, standing near Dru and her Aunt Dora at the top of the stairs, gave Dru's arm a little pinch. As he approached, she said prettily, "Aunt, this is the Viscount Wittimore, who is a friend of Lady Dartney's. Lord Wittimore, my aunt, Lady Channing; and my cousin, Miss Channing. How good of you to look in, sir."

He bowed. "How kind of you to invite me."

As he moved along, Esme said in an undertone to Dru, "Now that you have met him, you'll be able to present him to Lydia. I think you may find her in the dining hall. Run along and pitch her the tale."

With a look of acute discomfort, Dru did as she was told.

The musicians hired for the evening were by no means to be despised and, though the party was not a huge one, it was quite a gay affair.

It was with a feeling of intense satisfaction that Esme saw the viscount and Lydia conversing, though on closer inspection it seemed to her that Lydia was somewhat abstracted as she gazed about, probably trying to locate Kit—who was making himself as scarce as possible.

On quick steps, Esme made her way toward them. She tapped Lord Wittimore's arm playfully with her fan and said as archly as possible, "Let me tell you again how pleased I am that you could join us tonight, my lord, for I vow I told my cousins so much about you that they would have been fair disappointed if you had not put in an appearance."

"Indeed, you are too kind," he said with a cold smile, and then he turned to Lydia. "I believe this is our dance, is it not?" and bore her away with him. After one rather startled glance at her partner, Lydia could not forbear to cast a look of smug triumph at Esme.

Esme let out a long, satisfied breath. There! If seeing the viscount's clear preference for her over Esme and believing that she had cut her enemy out with a presentable male didn't predispose Lydia to friendly feelings toward St. John Wittimore, then nothing would.

In relief, Esme turned away to some of her own admirers and soon had the pleasure of having all her dances bespoken for the evening.

Though Lydia could not be said to display anything approaching flirtatiousness toward St. John Wittimore, still she did smile rather oftener than usual—a mistake with those teeth, thought Esme. However, Wittimore could not afford to be too nice in his distinctions, whatever her physical appearance. She stood up with him twice, and when Kit dawdled interminably, helping an elderly dowager from one part of the room to another while the company was drifting toward the dining hall, Lydia even allowed the viscount to take her in to supper.

With a very real sense of sacrifice, Esme forbore to eat supper with Captain Kendall and directed him to partner Verena instead and to take her to the group where there were two vacant places beside Kit.

"Well," Esme declared to her cousins after the party was over, "I do think Lydia is off to a promising start. Wittimore scarcely took his eyes off of her. I'm sure he must have been convinced I was telling the truth about her fortune, for he must have realised no one so lacking in charm as Lydia could have so good an opinion of herself unless she was very plump in the purse."

It was not many days later when St. John Wittimore

presented himself at the Channing house in Hanover Square, the drawing room of which was already crowded with other morning callers. As Lady Channing was sitting with three of her cronies and Dru was deep in conversation with several of her admirers, Esme crossed to Lord Wittimore, holding out her hand and with a little question in her eyes.

"Perhaps you would like to sit over here by the window," she suggested, gesturing to a nook fairly far removed from the other occupants of the room. "Now we can have a cosy visit."

"That is just what I would like, Miss Leonardo," the viscount said, though when they had settled themselves, he gave her a penetrating look but did not speak immediately.

"May I open my mind to you?" he asked at last.

"I wish you would," Esme said frankly and then quickly added, "What are friends for? And I hope you count me your friend."

"I do indeed, and as it was you who first extolled Miss Milliman's virtues to me, I'm sure she must count you as friend, too."

Esme dropped her eyes. "I'm sure I hope so," she said demurely.

"I hardly know how to frame the words, but in short, I have formed a lasting attachment toward Miss Milliman."

"Oh, happy couple!" Esme breathed. "How fortunate you both are."

"Well, I do believe we are well suited; however, perhaps the course of true love never did run smooth," he said in gloomy accents.

"You have not quarrelled?" she asked anxiously.

"No, no, I would not be such a fool—that is to say, I would not be so foolish as to disagree with any of Miss Milliman's opinions, as she is a remarkably sensible girl with a well-formed mind."

"Oh, remarkably," Esme echoed. "Then what is the problem?"

"I am by no means certain that she returns my sentiments."

"You must be more optimistic," Esme said bracingly. "Never have I observed her to show so marked a preference for anyone as she has shown you." It was fortunate that Esme did not have as high a regard for the truth as she did for the ends which justified the means, for she felt no twinge of conscience as she spoke these mendacious words.

The viscount brightened perceptibly for an instant, then a frown creased his brow. "And yet when I hinted to her that I was of a mind to speak to her father on a most important matter, she seemed to shy away and become almost cold."

"Lord Wittimore," Esme said earnestly, "while I am not wholly in Miss Milliman's confidence—" this much was certainly the truth—"still I believe I can interpret her reaction. As I told you, she is no hey-go-mad girl. I believe she cannot yet trust the violence of her own feelings. You have known each other for so short a time, after all. My best advice is to press your suit with *her*, but on no account speak to her father until she has given her consent for you to do so. She is the apple of his eye, and if he senses the least doubt in her, I cannot prophesy a happy outcome. In short, I do not believe you will succeed with *him* until he is convinced that she is sure of her own heart, and I believe some effort will yet be needed on your part to convince *her*. And yet surely the game is worth the candle, in view of Miss Milliman's undeniable assets."

"Yes," he said soberly. "It is indeed," and shortly afterward he bowed himself away.

Sir Henry Baillie and his wife, whose daughter was a debutante this Season, were a pleasant sort of couple, ordinary in every respect save for their mutual ambition to be thought unconventional. To that end, Sir Henry had built his house in Chelsea, a large square house with gardens sloping down to the river, and Lady Baillie had furnished it in a stridently Chinese style, which was very uncomfortable but well worth the discomfort because many of their guests on seeing it commented, "How striking!" or "How unusual!"

On the occasion of the first visit to Baillie Wick (as they whimsically called their house) of Mr. Alton Presteign, who was well known for his exquisite taste, he had murmured, "Only someone with your particular sense of colour, Lady Baillie, would have thought of combining this shade of purple with crimson." and though his mama had given him a sharp look, Lady Baillie had treasured the remark and ever afterward had thought of herself as someone who had a particular sense of colour.

When they gave a party for their daughter Beatrix that Season, of course it had to be something a little out-of-the-ordinary style, so they had the party conveyed down the river in boats to their house, with an orchestra playing on the lawn to welcome them. Luncheon was served in a pagoda-shaped tent, and fortunately the day was fine so that the guests were able to wander about the garden admiring the flowers and playing at lawn bowls.

The Channings and all their contemporaries were there, and Esme had just finished a glass of lemonade when she heard her cousin Kit saying to his friend Mr. Catchpole, "Jack, I've just been warned that that fellow in the puce velvet coat is a poet and he's going to treat us to a reading of some of his poems. I noticed that there's a little covered arbour with a comfortable bench down in the rose garden where we can't be seen. Care to join me?"

His friend groaned. "Not a hope. Lady Baillie is my godmama, you know. She would be sure to notice my defection."

"Well, I'm not going to stay and listen. Fellow's a manmilliner."

Out of the corner of her eye, Esme saw Lydia, who had been standing near enough to hear Kit's remarks, slip away and disappear down the path toward the rose garden. She stepped to Kit's side. "Cousin, I've another warning for you. I believe Lydia just overheard your remarks and has hurried off to hide herself in the arbour, so you must choose whether you would prefer that to the poet."

He gave her a look filled with dismay. "Thank you, Esme. Do you know, I have just discovered in myself a love for poetry I didn't know I possessed."

Before Lady Baillie had the opportunity of rounding up her guests for the reading, Esme slipped off to follow after Lydia.

That young lady was sitting on the bench in the arbour in an artful pose, a single rosebud clasped between her fingers, staring at it with rapt intensity. When she heard footsteps approaching and then stop before her, she paused a moment before lifting her eyes. "You!" A spasm of irritation crossed her face, ruining the picture she had so carefully prepared for Kit.

"It's lovely here, isn't it?" Esme said. "I could contemplate the roses forever. May I join you?" Without waiting for an answer, she sat down.

Lydia gathered her skirts around her. "I was just on the point of leaving."

Esme held out her hand. "Oh, do stay a moment, Miss Milliman—or may I call you Lydia, as my cousins do? There is something I have particularly wanted to say to you."

Lydia wrinkled her brow in a kind of disdainful surprise. "Yes?"

"I should tell you that since it was I who invited Lord Wittimore to our rout—where he met you—he has counted me his friend. Poor fellow, because he is almost wholly overset, he let slip in conversation with me the hope that lay nearest to his heart, and his great torment on learning from you that he must remain silent."

"Indeed." Lydia's tone was frosty, and yet she did not seem wholly displeased that Esme had learned of the viscount's devotion. "I had no idea he had made you his confidante."

"I believe that when one feels an emotion as keenly as Lord Wittimore does, it is almost impossible to suppress it entirely."

Lydia gave a little simper of gratification, but she said, "I'm afraid that he must suppress it. I should hardly like to have my name coupled with his and bruited about in society."

"I have wanted to tell you how much I admire you, Lydia."

Startled at this unexpected intelligence, Lydia cast a sideways glance of query at Esme.

"Yes, I admire you greatly," Esme went on, "for denying him the right to speak his heart, though one can imagine what your natural inclination would be from observing the way you seem to bloom in the presence of his devotion. Yes, you are admirable to give up a title as distinguished as that of the Viscountess Wittimore—the opportunity to be mistress of an illustrious estate such as Gurnstone—and settle for being merely Mrs. Channing of an indifferent farm like Tydings, and all because of a duty to your father's whim. You are indeed a dedicated daughter. I only hope your father appreciates your sacrifice, and that society will recognise your worth in foregoing worldly ambition in order to satisfy your father's wishes."

"Well, I hope I do know my duty," Lydia said, but she could apparently not bear her enemy's pity and so went on. "However, my case is not so sad as you present it, nor my papa so unreasonable. You do not take into consideration, I perceive, that your cousin Kit is heir to the Marquis of Locklynde and that I will one day be a marchioness." There was a triumphant little gleam in her eyes.

So! Lydia was not going to allow herself to be tempted by Lord Wittimore. Esme stared at her for a moment and then rose to pace agitatedly up and down the path. What was she to do? She could not bear to see all her fine plans come to nothing. Where could she ever find another titled gentleman with a great enough need for money and enough patience to court Lydia? It was too tiresome of Lydia to cling like a limpet to the notion of becoming Marchioness of Locklynde one day. But suppose she had reason to think that Kit would not inherit the title after all? Then Wittimore's importunings would sound a great deal sweeter to her ears. Impulsively, she turned. "Oh, my dear Lydia. I know you are above worldly considerations such as those, but I hope your father will not be too disappointed."

"What can you mean?" Lydia cried.

"Only that if he places his expectations on Kit's inheriting his cousin's title—well, I would not speak of it except that, in spite of our past differences, I cannot bear to see you forego the fate you so richly deserve because of your father's ambitions. In short, Kit is unlikely to inherit the title because . . . the Marquis of Locklynde is soon to take a wife."

She was a little astonished at her own daring, but the effect on Lydia was instantaneous. She sprang to her feet. "I do not believe it! There has been no announcement of such a thing. What can *you* know of the marquis's intentions?"

"Oh, my dear Lydia, there is no one who should *better* know his intentions. Need I say more? Indeed you must not press me, for *no one* is yet to know."

"What can you possibly mean?"

"May I swear you to secrecy?"

Lydia stiffened. "I cannot imagine any secrets you and I might share."

"Still, there is something—which I never thought to speak of yet—that I think you should know."

"Something concerning the marquis's plans that you are privy to? I hardly think it likely!" Her tone was scornful.

Esme's eyes flashed. "How odd that you should not have guessed. What should be more likely than that he and I should be acquainted? He frequents the great cities of

Europe, including my former home of Milan. Our families are connected in that I am cousin on my mother's side to his cousins, the Channings. When he was in the vicinity, it was quite natural that he should call upon my father.''

"And confided in you his marriage plans!" Lydia scoffed.

It was perhaps reprehensible, Esme reflected, but she felt no compunction at all in telling such plumpers to Lydia. All she could consider was that it might help free her cousin Kit from a detestable obligation which was bound to ruin his happiness. And Lydia was such a prig, staring down her nose in scorn as if Esme were less than nobody!

"First, you must promise that no word of this shall pass your lips," she cautioned.

Looking extremely piqued, Lydia made the vow.

"My father was not at all well when the marquis first called upon us. Locklynde was all kindness, coming again and again to render my father such services as could make him comfortable and easy in his mind. I cherished his consideration for my beloved parent, but as we grew to be closer and closer friends, I was unprepared for the true state of my—and his—feelings. In short, we tumbled into love!"

Lydia gave a shriek of protest.

"Yes," Esme said, her eyes sparkling as she embroidered the tale. "Unfortunately, the state of my father's health was so precarious we dared not broach the subject, fearing that any strong emotion, whether joy or distress, might prove fatal to him. We could not be sure he would approve the match. He liked Locklynde very well, but would he be able to bear with fortitude parting from his only child? Would he think Locklynde too old for me? We delayed until my father should grow stronger, but alas—that happy day never came. And then came the part that I cannot expect anyone of your high principles to approve—we entered into a secret betrothal.

"I was underage, and my uncle Frederick was now my guardian. Locklynde needed to apply to him for my hand.

72

We could, of course, not properly marry so soon after my father's death, so Locklynde remained on the Continent to take care of various business enterprises in which he is engaged. However, as soon as he returns to England and secures my uncle's permission, our formal betrothal and marriage will quickly follow."

Lydia had grown more and more flushed of face during this artful recital. Now she burst out, "I do not believe you!"

Esme managed a bewildered look. "But Lydia, why should I tell you such a thing if it weren't true? What would I possibly have to gain? My only reason for sharing with you a secret to which even my cousins are not privy is to save you from throwing over Lord Wittimore out of obedience to your father. And if the reason for your father's desiring your match with Kit is the expectation that he will inherit the title, then I thought you should know the truth. If you truly love Kit and will be happy as a simple farmer's wife then, by all means, have him. I only thought that if you did have a sincere *tendre* for the viscount—as he has for you—then you should be aware of the situation. You must let your heart dictate.

"And now I must take my leave. I believe my cousins will be wondering where I have taken myself off to." And with that, she ran down the path, leaving Lydia behind, her mouth gaping impotently like a beached fish.

It was not until Esme was halfway back to the house that she stopped stock-still and pressed her hands to her cheeks. "My God, what have I done?" she gasped. How could she have gotten so carried away as to tell Lydia that when the marquis returned to England, he would call upon her Uncle Frederick and ask permission to marry her? Because he *had* returned! Drusilla had seen him driving in the park. But he must have gone away again, as nothing more had been heard of him. Her aunt was sure he had taken himself out of the vicinity. Oh, if he were down on his estate, Esme begged a merciful Providence, let him stay there. Or even better, let him at this very moment be frequenting some gaming hall in Austria or Prussia. How dreadful if her wild tale should come to his ears!

Then she took herself sternly in hand. *Corragio!* she whispered. After all, Lydia had sworn a solemn vow of silence. And even if by dreadful mischance the marquis were still in England and returned to London, his path and Lydia's would be most unlikely to cross, would they not? Of course they would. She was quite safe, she assured herself. And if Lydia believed her story, she would surely think twice before refusing St. John Wittimore.

Esme could scarcely contain herself in patience until she might learn whether her tale to Lydia had borne fruit.

There was a ball the next night, and when the two young ladies came face to face, Lydia's eyes bore glitteringly into Esme's for a moment before she turned to continue her conversation with her partner. Lydia danced twice with Lord Wittimore, and while his expression did not betoken ecstasy, neither did he seem sunk in gloom. However, she danced with Kit also. Perhaps, Esme thought, she was as yet unable to make up her mind, but as long as she had not refused the viscount, there was still hope, for he would be unlikely to turn his attentions from her—unless a richer catch swam into view.

Having satisfied herself that she had done as much as she could for the moment, she devoted herself to having a very good time, flirting in an off-hand way with several of her own casual beaux and wondering once again if she could work herself up to the pitch of feeling a positive *tendre* for the delightful Captain James Kendall.

The one shadow on her evening was that Dru was practically hanging upon Sidney Porterfield's every word, and Esme could not but think she was throwing herself away if she should bestow her heart in *that* direction, despite Mr. Porterfield's good looks. Sir Edwin Childress or Lord Bartling were much more worthy of Dru's regard, Esme could not help feeling, and both of them were obviously captivated by Dru. Well, perhaps she could turn her attention that way when the business with Lydia was settled.

=== 7 ===

NOT MANY DAYS later, Esme entered the sacred portals of Almack's, feeling in especially prime twig. Her coral-coloured ball gown was new and very becoming. Her dark curls were twisted high on her head with a pearl fillet and with just a few locks escaping to fall loose and frame her face.

The hour was not yet so very advanced when a newcomer entered the ballroom and caught her attention. He was tall, with wide shoulders, very dark eyes and hair, and a saturnine face. He was dressed all in stark black save for his snowy waistcoat and cravat. His coat might have been moulded to his form. Esme knew she had not seen him before. He was beyond the age of most of the young bucks who frequented the Marriage Mart to look over its wares, and there was nothing in his somewhat forbidding expression to indicate he was the sort of man who would find amusement in the insipid refreshments or the chicken-stakes card games offered by Almack's.

Before she could speculate further, her presence was claimed by her partner for the set just forming.

It was warm in the room, and when the set was over Esme, waiting for her partner to procure a glass of lemonade for her, was fanning herself with a very pretty nile green fan, which matched her kid slippers. Suddenly she heard Lydia's voice behind her, saying in biting tones, "Here she is. Miss Leonardo, of course I need not introduce you to Lord Locklynde."

Esme stood absolutely rooted to the spot, her little fan arrested mid-wave, as colour rushed into her face.

"*Miss Leonardo*," a commanding voice spoke.

Slowly she turned and, with downcast eyes, blindly held out her hand. She felt it taken in a strong masculine one, felt lips touch her fingers and a sort of shock ripple along her nerves. Actually to *kiss* a lady's hand was no longer even in fashion, not in England, and this kiss was a lingering, insolent one. A sense of outrage stiffened her courage, and she looked up into the glittering dark eyes of the stranger she had seen earlier. The wicked marquis! She shivered just a little. The eyes were unfathomable, but whatever they held, it was not gentleness nor good will.

A firm hand took her elbow. "If you will excuse us, Miss Milliman, the lady and I have much to discuss." Feeling as if she were being marched to her doom, Esme followed the marquis's insistent lead. "*Coraggio!*" she whispered to herself. At the door of an anteroom he paused, and the young blade in possession of it took one look at the marquis's face and decided he had pressing business elsewhere. Locklynde seated Esme on a small couch.

Willing her lips not to tremble, she said in a tone of artificial brightness, "I have heard my cousins speak of you often, my lord, but as you have not called upon my aunt, I did not know you were in London. This is indeed a surprise."

"Yes? Well, let us say that before my betrothal is puffed off in the *Times*, I thought I should not do less than make the acquaintance of my future bride."

Her eyes flew to his face. She was so angry that even the deep irony she saw there could not frighten her out of speaking her mind. "Lydia! And she gave me her word she would not tell a soul! Well, that just shows you she is not to be trusted!"

"Do I understand that you told Miss Milliman we were betrothed?"

Esme nodded.

"And now you accuse *her* of untrustworthiness?" There was heavy sarcasm in his voice.

"Well, I know you must wonder why I should have done such a thing—" she began.

"Indeed," he murmured.

"It was all quite your fault."

"My fault?" Now she had surprised him a little.

"Yes, it was, for being so high-handed as to insist that Kit marry her when you have never interested yourself enough to find out what is best for him."

"Kit? You are speaking of Christopher Channing? Why the devil should I care whom the young puppy marries?"

She stared at him. "Well, of all the infamous—do you mean to say you don't even remember upholding my uncle's edict that he must marry Lydia Milliman?"

A spasm of irritation crossed his face. "Oh, your Uncle Hasborough. I daresay he did apply to me about some such case. The boy was shockingly volatile, I believe. I had had to go to considerable trouble to pull him out of one scrape, and his uncle feared that if he didn't settle down, it would be the same story again."

"Oh, this surpasses anything!" Esme cried. "*You* call Kit volatile! All *he* did was write some foolish letters a long time ago. *He* did not elope or get into a duel and have to flee the country and—"

"Yes, yes, that will be quite enough ancient history," his lordship said, scowling. "You have failed to make clear why you informed Miss Milliman there was an engagement between us."

"Because she only wants to marry Kit for the sake of the title. She is rich, but her aunt is called 'Lady,' you see, and her cousins are Honourables. And Uncle Frederick wishes for the match in order to get hold of a piece of land that will be part of her dowry, as well as being a good friend of Mr. Milliman. It's one of those foolish notions that has been held for years by Lydia's parents and my uncle. Well, to give him his due, my cousin Dru confided to me that my uncle himself had married for love and the match did not turn out happily. His wife was fickle, I believe. Possibly, he wishes to save Kit from a similar disaster because certainly no one could ever imagine Lydia playing her husband false, or even having the opportunity of doing so. But Kit does not care for her at all. However, he is so beholden to his uncle that if he doesn't obey and offer for her, his mama will probably be so cast down into guilt that she will feel bound to leave her brother's home where she is so very comfortable. Then what will become of Dru and Hope and Constance? And if, instead of agreeing that Kit must marry Lydia and threatening to cut off his allowance just as he is trying his utmost to get Tydings back to a paying proposition, you had had the good sense to—"

Here she paused for breath, and he held up a hand. "If you think you are clarifying matters, you are fair and far out. I think you must be all about in the head. For the moment, let us forego Mr. Milliman's piece of land and Hasborough's unfortunate marriage and my aunt's guilt and Kit's efforts with Tydings. You lead off this plaguey faradiddle with the statement that Miss Milliman wishes to marry Kit for his title. Unless the Regent has granted him one since my last visit to England, which I should think most unlikely, Kit doesn't have a title."

"Oh, it is *your* title she is anticipating."

"The devil—" he exclaimed most improperly. His face was such a mixture of stupefaction and outrage that she let out a sudden peal of laughter. And as she thought of her cousins' solemn predictions that the marquis could not be expected to sustain life for so very many years because of his dissipated habits, her amusement quite undid her because this man seated beside her, though there were lines of hard living in his face, looked as healthy a physical specimen as she could imagine. His tight-fitting coat showed no fat, only lean taut muscles; his eye was clearer than that of many men ten years younger; and his hand on her elbow had been as strong as iron.

"When you can control your mirth—" His voice cut coldly across her laughter. She gave another little choke and wiped her eyes.

"It is too absurd, my lord, but my cousins have taken it into their heads—and apparently so have the Millimans, though I have of course never discussed it with *them*—that you are past praying for. They think that someone of your dissipated habits is bound to be run through with a sword or shot with a duelling pistol at an early date or, failing that, that drinking and gambling and wenching will carry you off instead, though—" and here she had to pause to get her voice under control again—"though Dru allows that you *may* linger for years."

After a moment of stunned silence he said, "I see," with an odd note in his voice. "And does Kit wish for my early demise as well?"

"Oh no, of course he does not *wish* for it at all. It is like a doom hanging over his head. If it weren't for the wretched title, Lydia wouldn't wish to marry him, and he would be free to marry where he pleases. But though he doesn't wish for it, he believes the nonsense. How such a notion got started I can't imagine, but they are all convinced of it."

"And had it never occurred to any of my loving relations that I might present an heir who would cut Kit out?"

"*Exactly* what I said," Esme cried, pleased to find him quick of intellect. "But—" and here another gale of mirth overcame her—"this is the cream of the jest, they do not look for any *legitimate* issue because they believe you are not so lost to all sense of what you owe your name that you would *marry* one of your bits of muslin, and they think no *lady* would have you, so steeped in vice as you are."

He looked completely taken aback by this intelligence. Then he said stiffly, "I'm pleased that my depraved situation affords you such amusement."

"I don't know how they can all be such gudgeons," she said gaily. "I suppose it is from living so deep in the country. But it surpasses understanding how they can suppose that anyone with a title so high as marquis and a fortune in the bargain could not find a wife of suitable family at the mere snap of his fingers! Why, in any Season I suppose there must be quite a dozen impoverished gentlemen of good birth trying to marry their daughters to a high bidder."

"Thank you," he said with deep irony. "Your faith in my ability to marry respectably is a great comfort."

"Of course, they really doubt that you would care to bother with a wife at all at this late stage in your life."

"Amazing how you can raise my spirits one moment only to dash them the next. It does strike me that for a delicately nurtured young female, your conversation is improper beyond reckoning and your outlook cynical."

"Cynical? Oh no. Really?" She looked interested. "Is it truly? I expect that comes of having lived abroad and among artists for so long, which is not *quite* the same as being delicately nurtured. But I really don't think my language is improper. It is you who keep using words like 'devil.' "

"I beg pardon," he said with exaggerated politeness.

"Oh, I expect the provocation was great when you did not perfectly understand *why* I told Lydia that we were secretly betrothed. It is her fault the story came out, and most vexatious. Naturally, I did not expect it to come to your ears. Well, how could I dream of such a thing when you were not even in London, and she promised not to tell anyone?"

"I can see that Miss Milliman is perfidious beyond anything. Still, I do not perfectly understand the news of our betrothal."

At this moment, they were interrupted by the sight of

Lady Channing in the doorway, her turban slightly askew. "Good God, then it's true! I was told that Esme was closeted with you—"

"Hardly closeted, Aunt Dora." The marquis rose and bowed over her hand.

"Locklynde, I did not know you were back in England. And how did you meet my niece?"

"I have been waiting with some impatience for her to reach that point in the story myself," he said.

"What do you mean?" A puzzled line creased Lady Channing's brow. "Well, never mind. This won't do at all. Come along, Esme; our carriage is ordered."

"I will wait upon you tomorrow," he said with chilling emphasis, his eyes on Esme's face.

There was no denying that Miss Esme Leonardo spent an uncomfortable night. Of all the unfortunate starts that her words to Lydia should come to the marquis's ears! He could spoil everything—and just when she was so hopeful of a happy outcome.

It took a great deal of resolution for her to face the day that lay ahead, but to her relief, the drawing room was fairly packed with callers the next morning. Captain James Kendall was there, his amusing nonsense giving her courage, though she listened to him half-abstractedly. Mr. Sidney Porterfield was also among the visitors, along with several other of Drusilla's swains, and half a dozen of Lady Channing's cronies.

The latter were agog to know what had brought Locklynde back to England and what he had been saying to Esme, but as Lady Channing did not know the answer to either of these questions, their curiosity bid fair to go unsatisfied.

An expectant hush fell over the room at the butler's announcement, "Lord Locklynde." He strode in, looking formidable in his coat of wine-coloured superfine, his dove grey pantaloons, and modishly austere cambric shirt. The impatience on his saturnine features when he saw the crowded room soon turned to boredom at the twittering inanities uttered to him.

Esme had put on one of her more conservative dresses of pomona green with a striped spencer, as if in hopes of escaping notice. In this she was disappointed. When the marquis had had all of the small talk he was willing to bear, and a great deal more than he had wished to hear, he bowed to Lady Channing and said, "I must take my leave of you, ma'am. I have called in to take Miss Esme driving."

An alarmed silence followed this announcement, and then she stammered, "Well, I—if you—if Esme—" and at this point, Esme decided she may as well get it over with and said quietly, "I'll just get my things."

She took her time fastening her pelisse and tying her bonnet. If one were about to have one's head bitten off, one might as well be looking one's neatest, though she hardly thought that a fetching bonnet would distract his lordship.

The groom had been walking his horses, a magnificent pair of bays. The marquis, now arrayed in a many-caped driving coat and curly beaver hat, handed her into the elegant curricle, and they set off at a spanking pace.

"I believe that when we were interrupted," he remarked, "you were just on the point of explaining why you put it about that we were betrothed."

"I did *not* put it *about*!" Esme said with a flash of spirit. "I told no one but Lydia and not until I had extracted her solemn vow she would not repeat it."

"Which shows she is not trustworthy; I know that part. Go on." His voice was implacable.

"I would not have done it had it not been necessary. You see, though we all talked a deal of nonsense about ridding ourselves of Lydia by somewhat gothic means, it seemed to me that the only feasible way to manage it was to induce Lydia to choose someone else. And there wasn't much time. Her family was willing that she should have a Season first, and Kit cannot quite afford a wife yet, but it will not be long before Uncle Frederick will apply more pressure on him to make the thing official. The problem was that I had to find someone Lydia would accept—which meant a title—and someone who would accept Lydia as well, and that was the hard part because she is not exactly—well, if you knew her well, you would understand. I cannot describe what it is about her manner, but no one could imagine a dashing, titled young blade choosing her from the field. I thought the simplest thing would be if she married you directly—then she could have the title without waiting for Kit to inherit.''

He choked slightly and then, ''I see,'' he said dryly. ''And had you formed a plan to convince me to choose a bride that no dashing blade would have had?''

She blushed and turned away. ''Dru convinced me that it would not serve.''

''I must remember to express my gratitude to my cousin Drusilla.''

''Well, I only thought it might be possible because if you *did* wish to set up your nursery, you probably would not forsake your old habits anyway, and Lydia could not be so very much of a burden down on your estate while you were off pursuing other pleasures.''

''Your thoughtfulness in providing me with a wife who is not *very* much of a burden almost unmans me.''

She winced a little at his ironic tone but made a quick recovery. ''Well, I gave up that plan. Several other candidates did not work out either. But then I made the acquaintance of Lord Wittimore, and he seemed perfect in every respect. You see, he's a bona fide fortune hunter, but he *is* a viscount, and Lady Dartney assured me it's a very old title. His estate is distinguished enough to appear in the guidebooks, too, and Lydia should like that. The thing was, it had to be done quickly before Lydia discovered he hadn't a feather to fly with and only needed an heiress because his house was falling to pieces and he had inherited a mountain of debts. And it did seem to be working out. She enjoyed the attentions he paid her, for heaven knows she could hardly have found Kit an ardent suitor. And it was obvious she was tempted. After all, she could be a viscountess *now* instead of having to wait to become a marchioness."

"While I lingered on?" he inquired pleasantly.

She frowned at his facetiousness. "Still, it would be much grander to be a marchioness, besides her father being such a particular friend of Kit's uncle. I was afraid she was going to turn Lord Wittimore away. So it was apparent that there was only one thing I could do—tell her that you were on the point of marriage, because I knew she did not want Kit for himself—only for the title, and if it looked as if he wouldn't get the title, then she might accept Lord Wittimore before he became discouraged and looked further for an heiress."

"Your machinations have a masterful touch, Esme. Once free of Lydia, Kit would be able to take a bride of his own choosing; is that correct?"

"Exactly." She was pleased that she had made the picture clear at last.

For a few moments, he seemed to be concentrating on manoeuvring his bays past a showy phaeton driven by an indifferent whipster who was taking an unfair share of the path. Then he said, "Did it not occur to you that as Kit is my heir, I might thrust a spoke in his wheel if he chose someone of whom I could not approve?"

"Of course you could, but I did not think it likely you would interest yourself overmuch. After all, it was only at my Uncle Frederick's behest that you said he must not offer for anyone but Lydia. And if she were no longer available, why should you care whom he chose?"

"Since there is certainly the *possibility* that Kit will inherit the title, do you really think I would allow him to become leg-shackled to an unconscionable little liar?"

Esme gasped. "What an outrageous thing to say!"

He gave her a sidewise glance. "Is it?"

"You are totally unfair. I believe her to be all that is sweet and good, and as for your opinion—why, you have not even met her, I believe."

He looked startled. "Of whom are you speaking?"

"Why, of Verena Gaylord, of course. She is the girl Kit loves, and the match would be a most unexceptionable one."

He stared at her blankly, and she stared back, a mixture of bewilderment and indignation in her face. Then suddenly she gave a little cry. "Oh my! You could not have thought—you surely did not believe I wanted to save Kit from Lydia for—for myself!"

"The thought had just crossed my mind," he said dryly.

Colour rushed to Esme's cheeks. "How shabby you must think me—to scheme to win a husband by trickery."

"I believe it was not an unwarranted conclusion to draw," the marquis said.

"Well, I can see how you might think any girl would be attracted to him," she said, "for he is the handsomest thing, and so charming and sweet of nature, too, but it was clear from the outset that he wanted me for a sister. He was already hopelessly in love with Verena, you see. And though he is only my cousin, I think of him almost as the brother I never had, and I could not stand by while his real sisters did nothing but wring their hands and moan about the tragedy of it without making the least push to mend matters."

"If this is what you call the 'least push,' I should hate to see you take decisive action," he mused.

She turned accusing eyes on him. "You have quite misjudged my character if you think I would have plotted to gain such a match for myself—that *would* have been odious."

"Whereas to plot against Lydia for Miss Gaylord's sake is commendable," he commented.

"Well, I should not call plotting commendable, precisely," she admitted, "but it was necessary. I could not be so pudding-hearted as to allow such a dismal match if I could prevent it. If you knew Lydia better, you would see that she is not at all worthy of Kit. And if you had troubled to know *him* better, you would see that it is quite wicked that he should miss his chance of happiness—and Verena hers— simply because of other people's selfish whims.''

''I see that I have seriously wronged you,'' he said with utmost gravity in his voice.

''Well, you have,'' she agreed. ''I should not dream of plotting in my own behalf. And even if I were so inclined, I daresay it would be quite impossible. I do not expect to make a match at all. I only thought it would be very pleasant to have a Season—rather like having an unexpected gift that one doesn't know quite how one will use but which is too nice to throw away. And it seemed as if all the gaiety we are enjoying would be something interesting to look back on.''

He looked at her in a little surprise. ''Why didn't you expect to make a match?'' he inquired.

''Oh, well,'' she gestured as if the answer were patently obvious, ''I have no fortune, you see, only the merest pittance. So it would have to be some half-pay officer who fell mad enough in love with me to throw his cap over the windmill.'' She giggled a little at the notion. ''And with my complexion, I hardly think that's likely. They do say that brunettes are in favour this year, but a swarthy skin is never fashionable, I believe.''

He studied her countenance and wondered if she did not realise that her great speaking, sparkling dark eyes were enough to make many a man dismiss a peaches-and-cream complexion as insipid.

''And then of course there's Papa. He had enormous talent and gave pleasure to multitudes, but you know how starched-up the English are about performers of any sort, besides his being Italian. He was the son of a count, which possibly helps a little, even though the count was a very unpleasant sort who disowned Papa when he went on the operatic stage and would have disowned him again if such a thing were possible when he married my mama. I believe some Englishman cheated him in a business transaction once, and he detested the whole race from then on. He was very volatile. Well, so was Papa, but in *quite* a different way, and he never bore grudges. And it was the right life for him because he adored opera and loathed growing grapes, so he was never the least bit sorry. And neither am I, except for knowing that it would make marriage to a gentleman most unlikely. Indeed, were it not that my Aunt Dora's credit is so very good, I'm sure I would not be received in society at all, and her procuring me the voucher for Almack's was the greatest stroke of luck. Lady Cowper is an old friend of my aunt's, and she knew my mama years ago and thought her a very nice girl.''

"I think you have taken too gloomy a view of your situation," he said.

"Oh, I am not sunk in gloom," she assured him in a practical tone. "I have thought to set myself up as a modiste, only that takes capital, so I believe I will apply to my old governess for a teaching post in her school. I'm good at languages and proficient enough on the pianoforte, and of course I sketch rather well.''

"But I thought your uncle had offered you a home," he said.

"Yes, and it has been a very pleasant few months," she said with a tiny catch in her voice. "I will always remember with gratitude the opportunity of being such great friends with my cousins. But I could hardly expect my uncle to allow me to stay when he discovers he has nursed a viper in his bosom.'' She turned her face away to hide the tiny tremble of her lips, as she did not want his pity.

He was silent for a few moments, and then he said abruptly, "This Sidney Porterfield who was making sheep's eyes at my cousin Drusilla—was that one of your schemes, too?''

She swung around to face him indignantly. "Of course not! How could you think such a thing?"

"My dear girl, how could I think otherwise?"

"Well, you are quite mistaken. In fact, I briefly considered him for Lydia because he will very likely be a baron one day, but when—"

"When what?" he prompted.

She squirmed nervously. She could not betray Dru's feelings to this high-handed tyrant, but he was plainly waiting for an answer. "Oh, I decided it would be ineligible."

"It is also ineligible for him to stand on terms of intimacy with anyone in my family."

"Indeed," she said coldly. "Then I suppose you must tell my aunt to bar her doors against him, though it will not be easy, for he is received everywhere. And I don't know that he is a fortune hunter—I only thought Lydia's money might be of use to him in his career, but if he is seriously dangling after Dru—and I don't know that he is—then he must not be hanging out for a rich wife after all."

"Perhaps there are other considerations," he said thoughtfully. And then, "It will not do. I shall expect you to bend every effort to see that it comes to nothing."

"Me?" she said in surprise. "Why should you suppose I might be able to influence the course of their friendship?"

"You seem to be an expert at schemes."

She gave an indignant little bounce. "I told you—only when it's in a very good cause. And I don't see that it's any of your concern if Dru should happen to like Mr. Porterfield. It's outside of enough that you have tried to ruin Kit's life, without interfering in Dru's."

It occurred to her to wonder why she was defending Mr. Porterfield when she privately thought Dru would be throwing herself away on him, despite his being very handsome, and decided it was that she resented the marquis's high-handed manner. She stole a look at his implacable face and then said rather defiantly, "Anyway, I couldn't help you even if I chose because I shall doubtless be turned out in disgrace when my uncle discovers I told Lydia we were betrothed.''

He gave a condescending nod to two gaping matrons passing down the path in a smart equipage and then said, "There's no doubt you have landed yourself in a scrape, but it need not be a fatal one. Supposing I did not completely disavow this faradiddle?''

She was totally dumbfounded. "What can you mean?''

"Why, that I might go to your uncle and tell him we had met abroad and formed a regard for one another but that because of your youth and our long separation, I feel that we should become reacquainted and that I would like his permission to pay my addresses to you until such time as we determine whether your heart is truly engaged. If we are seen to go about together, that should silence Lydia's tongue.''

Her mouth formed an O of astonishment. "But why should you do such a thing?''

"Let us say that the milk of human kindness runs freely in my breast.''

"Let us not say anything so absurd. *Belle parole non pascon i gatti.* Fine words do not feed cats,'' she said with narrowed eyes. "You have some scheme in mind.''

"Well, if anyone would recognise a schemer—'' he murmured.

"Besides, Uncle Frederick would hardly like such an arrangement. It is not in his interest that you marry.''

His face darkened in scorn. "What the devil should I care what your uncle likes? Do you really think I would let such a one as Frederick Hasborough stand in my way?''

She shivered a little, looking at his scornful expression. At this moment, she could believe that the wicked marquis would not let anyone stand in his way. High-handed tyrant! And yet, if for whatever reason he would substantiate her claim, just long enough for Lydia to relinquish Kit and tie herself to Wittimore. . . . But he frightened her a little because she sensed some dark purpose in him. Perhaps it would be better simply to make a clean breast of the thing to her uncle and accept her banishment.

He sensed her hesitation and said, "Come, you showed no want of spirit earlier. Why do you shy from taking the fence now? Perhaps you are right about Lydia and I should learn to know her better before I condemn Kit to marriage with her. If she thinks that we will marry and throws Kit over because of it, then you will be proved right that she cares only for the title."

"Yes, but meanwhile—" she began, and shivered again.

"Meanwhile you will be condemned to spend some time in my company, which I can see is a horrid fate in itself, as well as scaring off all your half-pay officers, but I remind you, it is your scheme after all. Come, what shall it be; courtship from a wicked *elderly* marquis, or confessing to your own lies?"

"This is blackmail," she said, "and I don't see your purpose. *Non intendo.*"

"It is not necessary for you to understand me," he said sternly, "but merely to make up your mind."

She took a deep breath and sat up very straight. "Very well," she said with sudden resolution. "The courtship it will be, but *don't*, I beg you, let us have any more nonsense about the milk of human kindness. You have some dark purpose of your own for doing this."

He gave her a strange little half smile, hardly more than a twitch of his lips. "But meanwhile, the pretence will serve to save your pretty little neck."

She put a hand on her throat, as though she could almost imagine it laid on the chopping block. Locklynde whipped up the horses and turned to go back to Hanover Square.

=8=

"WELL, YOU ARE a sly one," her uncle said in a peevish tone as he met Esme in the drawing room before dinner, "never telling us you were so well acquainted with Locklynde."

Esme dropped her eyes and twisted her handkerchief. Then, inventive as always, she said, "You see, he could have changed his mind, sir. It has been a long time since we last met. My mind had such a melancholy cast after Papa died that I fancied perhaps the marquis's regard for me was based partly on pity. If after we parted he had preferred to forget our understanding, I would have been humiliated if I had told you about it."

"No one on your *mother's* side of the family would be capable of such deceit," he said, apparently overlooking the fact that Esme's mama had all but eloped with her opera singer and very likely would have done, had her father not capitulated and given his consent.

Esme blushed but could scarcely defend herself against the charge of deceit, though the deception was quite a different one from what her uncle took it to be.

"He's quite unsuitable for you," he said reprovingly. "He's nearly twice your age, and the life he's led! I find myself astonished that your father would have allowed you to become acquainted with him. Though perhaps I should not be surprised at anything an Italian opera singer would do."

Esme bit back an angry retort.

"He's more likely to ruin you than marry you," he said,

"and if you should manage to get him to the altar, you'd have cause to regret it. I cannot believe he would abandon his excesses to please *you*."

"I wonder then that you gave permission for him to pay his addresses to me," she said audaciously.

A red stain deepened on his pink scalp. Esme found herself recalling Locklynde's scornful tone as he predicted that her Uncle Frederick would not be able to stand against him and wondered what pressure he had brought to bear. Fortunately, at that moment her cousins entered the room, obviously unaware of what had passed between their uncle and the marquis, for they seemed quite as usual in their manners.

Dinner was an uncomfortable meal, however, as she often felt her Aunt Dora's eyes on her face and realised her Uncle Frederick must have confided the news to his sister. She could imagine that that good lady's feelings were in turmoil as she contemplated the possibility that her niece's match would cut her son out of the succession to the title of marquis. She wished she could explain the truth to her aunt —that it was all a sham—but she feared Lady Channing's sensibilities would be much too shocked.

They were engaged that evening for a play with some pleasant but very dull friends of Lady Channing's. Esme did not see Locklynde in any of the other boxes, but she steadfastly forbore to stroll about during the interval, for fear of meeting him.

She was just ready for bed when her door burst open and Dru, followed by Hope and Constance, entered unceremoniously. "Esme, you beast," Hope cried. "How could you let us go on and on about the wicked marquis as if you'd never heard of him, when all the time you were practically betrothed?"

"Mama just told us," Dru said in a reproachful tone, "and really, Esme, it was too bad of you."

"Well, I think it's like something in a novel," Constance said, "only I do think you might have told us."

Suddenly Esme fell into whoops at their indignant faces. "You silly geese never believed that tale! You *must* have known it was all a hum."

They stared at her in blank astonishment.

"You must swear—in blood—that you will not tell a soul," she cautioned. At their puzzled nods, she went on, "Of course I had never met Locklynde, but we agreed something had to be done to save Kit from Lydia, and it did seem to be working out well with Lord Wittimore, only he confided to me that Lydia was unwilling to allow him to speak to her papa. I was afraid he'd become discouraged and find himself another heiress. So it seemed to me that some action was necessary—no matter how drastic—to make Lydia decide to choose him over Kit. So—" she paused and then decided to get it over with in a rush—"I told her I was secretly betrothed to the marquis!"

"Esme! You never did!" Dru gasped.

"I think it was masterful," Connie said, "because Esme looks quite healthy enough to bear a dozen sons and cut Kit out."

"But what made her believe it?" Dru demanded.

"I'm not sure that she did completely," Esme admitted, "though I spun a very good tale. However, it gave her enough to think about that she kept Lord Wittimore as a second string to her bow. But that wretched creature, though she had sworn secrecy, traitorously repeated the story and I don't know in what quarters. However, I think whoever heard it must not have found it believable or it would have become the *on-dit* of the Season, which we know it is not or your mama would surely have heard it. But somehow it reached Locklynde's ears. I could kill Lydia, I vow."

With a dramatic groan, Hope dropped onto Esme's bed. "But he must have been furious."

"Well, I believe he was. I must admit I was ready to sink. Oh, if only he'd stayed out of England! But then—it's hard to explain—when he appeared and sat there so superior and top-loftly making sarcastic remarks, I became angry and pointed out that it was all his fault for insisting Kit marry Lydia, without troubling himself in the least to know if they would suit. I explained that *someone* had to save Kit because Lydia only wanted the title and that that was why I told her that Canterbury tale.''

''Esme, that was brave to the point of foolhardiness,'' Dru said. ''How could you speak so to a man like our cousin Jared?''

''Well, he could not eat me, after all, and not even *he* would run me through with a sword. I knew the worst he could do was deny the story and make me a laughingstock, and I'd be sent away in disgrace, but since that seemed bound to happen anyway, I thought he might as well hear a few home truths first.''

''But I don't understand,'' Hope frowned. ''Mama said he'd called on Uncle Frederick for permission to pay his respects to you.''

''That is the oddest part,'' Esme admitted with a puzzled frown. ''We fixed it up on our drive this morning. I had told Lydia that he called upon Papa in Milan and that is how we became friends. Only Papa had become too ill for us to discuss our future with him. And the marquis offered to confirm that story to our uncle, or most of it anyway—not that we were actually pledged, but that he held me in regard and believed I had returned his feelings, only because of my *youth* he wanted to give me time to be sure I really knew my own heart.'' She gave a whoop of laughter. ''He is *almost* as good at concocting tales as I am.''

Dru frowned her down. ''That is hardly something to boast of.''

''I think it's quite heroic of her,'' Hope said. ''None of *us* could think of a way to help Kit.''

''But, Esme,'' Constance wanted to know, ''*why* did Cousin Jared agree to get you out of this scrape?''

''I wish I could tell you,'' Esme said, frowning.

"You don't think we would betray you!" Hope said indignantly.

"No, of course not. I only meant I can't tell you because I don't know. And he didn't *agree* to it. I never would have dreamed of asking such a thing. Suddenly he just offered to do it."

"It doesn't sound at all like the sort of thing he would do," Dru said.

"I shouldn't have thought so either," Esme said. "He tried to bamboozle me that it sprang from the milk of human kindness, but when he saw *that* wouldn't fadge, he said that perhaps I was right about Lydia and that he wanted to observe her and see if it were true that she cared more for the title than for Kit." Here she looked very sober. "But I'll tell you what. *I* think he has some different purpose in mind that I can't begin to guess at. It frightens me a little. Perhaps he means to set me up so that everyone is talking about us, and then advertize the true story so that I'll be held in public ridicule. But if only he waits until Lydia is tied to Wittimore, that will be a small price to pay."

"Or perhaps he means to ruin you," Hope said sagely, unconsciously echoing her uncle's words. "That would be more in his style."

"Well, he'll catch cold at that," Esme declared with a display of bravado she was far from feeling. "I am not quite so green as everyone seems to think."

But when they had all left and she had slipped under her eiderdown, she gave a little shiver. That the Marquis of Locklynde was playing some deep game of his own, she was quite sure. And in any game he chose to play, she was certain he would prove a formidable opponent.

Though Dru was correct in that there were a number of mamas in London who took care to keep their innocent damsels away from the wicked marquis's eyes, not all doors in polite society were closed to him by any means. Indeed, there were more than a few youngish matrons who had been in his set when he had first come up to London a dozen years ago and who were disposed to regard him now with nostalgic, if slightly exasperated, affection. And of course there were always a few daring hostesses who regarded the addition of a confirmed rake to their guest lists as almost de rigueur.

Lady Hatcher, for instance, who was several years his senior but had never forgotten how, with his dark good looks he had set her pulses racing all those years ago merely by telling her once that her eyes had glints of moonlight in them, was pleased to invite him to her ball. As the Channings and Esme were also to be among the guests, it gave Locklynde the opportunity to escort the three ladies in his carriage. Since the two Channings were his aunt and cousin, his act did not generally serve to single out Esme as having been paid undue attention by him, and yet she was sure that Lydia Milliman, at least, was quite aware of their arrival together.

Esme had taken pains to look her best tonight in a green peau-de-soie gown trimmed with the elegant silver leaves carefully saved from one of her mama's ball dresses. Her slippers were of silver kid, and the gauze scarf arranged over her bare arms was shot with silver threads.

It had been quite pleasant, she had to admit to herself, to be bowled along in Locklynde's luxuriously appointed carriage at such a spanking pace, rather than in her Uncle Frederick's antiquated coach. And it had been pleasant too when, at the sight of the crest emblazoned on the door, the Hatcher footmen had jumped with such alacrity to hand the ladies down.

After they had made their way up the crowded staircase to greet their hostess, the marquis did not seem to single Esme out, save for standing up with her once in a cotillion. He was an excellent dancer and said several things that made her laugh, though half her attention was on Lydia, in an effort to gauge that young lady's mood.

It seemed to Esme that Lydia was rather more tight-lipped

than usual that evening, though she reflected that, considering Lydia's teeth, perhaps that did her no disservice.

Drusilla was looking charmingly as usual in white net over a blue satin underdress. She danced twice with Sir Edwin Childress and then, when it was time to go in to supper, Esme found to her surprise that Locklynde had managed with no seeming effort to arrange a group consisting of himself and her, Drusilla and Lord Bartling, Lydia and Kit. She could not be altogether pleased, for Lord Wittimore was of the company that evening and had given them a morose look as he passed where they were sitting. On the other hand, perhaps seeing Locklynde and Esme supping together would give Lydia something to think about.

Drusilla did not seem at first entirely happy with the arrangement either, but her manners were so good that she allowed Lord Bartling to draw her out, and he soon found his efforts rewarded with some very lively responses from her. The only one of the six who could be said to be completely sunk in gloom was poor Kit. He was polite to a fault, rising at once when Lydia declared she would like another ice, but there was a rather set look around his mouth and a bleakness in his eyes that Esme thought his cousin Jared could hardly fail to note.

Lydia seemed to divide her time between behaving in a self-confidently proprietary way toward Kit and keeping a watchful eye on the marquis's behaviour toward Esme. At one point, she commented with false solicitude, "I did not see you at Miss Dewhorst's ball last night, Lord Locklynde. I hope no indisposition kept you away."

Though he was well aware that Lydia must know the Dewhorsts were among those extremely proper types who had neither wish nor financial need to see their delicately nurtured daughter exposed to the practised wiles of a middle-aged libertine like himself, he merely smiled in an unperturbed way and said, "No; I am not acquainted with Miss Dewhorst and did not receive an invitation card."

Lydia could not forbear to press the point. "I suppose

debutantes of eighteen or so must seem a childish lot to one who has . . . travelled so widely. Do you plan to return to the Continent soon?''

"I will be sure that you are informed when my plans are formulated," he said gravely, causing her to redden up unbecomingly. "For the moment, however, I find myself well content to enjoy such pleasures of the Season as are open to me." He allowed his glance to rest for just a fraction of an instant on Esme's face and, though she recognised that it was only play-acting, the practised ease with which he had managed to make a mere glance seem almost a caress made her understand why some mamas took care to keep their daughters out of Locklynde's way.

Lydia was quiet for a little and seemed abstracted. Then, as if coming to a sudden decision, she said to the marquis, "We are holding a rout on Tuesday next. If you would not be bored, I shall be happy to have a card sent to you."

He bowed slightly and murmured, "I'm sure I shall not be bored."

By the time the supper was over, Esme was sure Locklynde must be beginning to have an inkling at least of how unsuitable a match would be between Kit and Lydia. She wondered if he had arranged the group with the object in mind of observing the two together. The thing that puzzled her most was why Lydia had invited Locklynde to her rout. Not for the pleasure of his company; of that she was sure.

On Tuesday night, wearing a simple crepe gown in her favourite jonquil shade, her dark curls pinned up at the sides with fresh yellow roses, Esme surveyed the company at the Millimans' rout. To have said the rooms were thin of company would have been an exaggeration, but the affair could scarcely have been termed a squeeze either.

The Milliman fortune might be great enough to assure that the family were leaders of society down in their quiet backwater in the country, but by the standards of the *ton*, Mr. Milliman was merely well to pass. Neither did he have a title. And Lydia's manner of complacent superiority had by no means won her scores of friends among the Season's crop of debutantes and town beaux.

Still, in addition to many of her parents' cronies and the perennial party-goers who will attend any function where a decent meal and adequate wines are likely to be served, there were enough good-natured young people who had accepted the invitation with the hope of being pleased at finding themselves in congenial company that Esme thought the evening might not be a total bore.

She was pleased to see Captain James Kendall across the room, and Dru was already surrounded by a group of her admirers, including Sir Edwin and Lord Bartling. Though Kit had reluctantly agreed to attend at his mother's bidding, all the while knowing full well he would not see Verena this night, Esme had the satisfaction of observing Lord Wittimore also making an entrance.

The Marquis of Locklynde had said nothing to Esme about whether or not he planned to attend, but rather late she heard whispers and saw heads turning and looked around to see him in the doorway. It was always thus when he put in an appearance. She could not judge whether it was the notoriety surrounding his name that caused heads to turn, or whether it was simply the force of his presence: the bold dark eyes, the strong-featured face, the mouth so often curved in a sardonic half smile and yet looking as if it could keep its secrets.

Lydia seemed inordinately pleased to see the marquis, Esme thought, puzzled. She was wearing a gown which Esme, with her unerring clothes sense, felt was ill-advised, the shade of blue too intense for Lydia's pallid colouring, the puffs and ruffles too many, the décolletage too low for Lydia's rather bony chest. But there was an air of excitement about Lydia tonight that made her seem more vivacious than usual.

Esme had danced once with Locklynde and twice with Captain Kendall when, toward the middle of the evening, a footman came and gave her the message that her aunt wished to see her in the library. She followed him and entered to find Captain Kendall standing at a reading table idly turning over the pages of a book of engravings. Of Lady Channing there was no sight.

"James!" Esme exclaimed in surprise. "Have you seen my aunt?"

"Why, I believe she is in the card room," he said.

"But I had a message she wanted to see me here."

"Well, she has not been here these past ten minutes while I have been waiting for you."

"Waiting for me? What made you think I would be coming here?"

A frown creased his brow. "I had a message that you wished to see me here."

"*Non intendo.* Perhaps this is someone's idea of a joke." She turned at once to the door and, to her annoyance, found that the footman must have closed it behind her and it was stuck. "I can't seem to get this door open," she said.

Captain Kendall tried the knob and pushed with his shoulder, then turned to her and said, "I don't believe it is stuck; I believe it's locked from the outside."

"Not a joke after all," Esme said thoughtfully. "Something a bit more malicious." She looked about the room and saw there was no other exit. There was, however, a heavily carved pianoforte. She gave a little exclamation. "You can sing, can you not?" she asked the captain.

He blinked in surprise. "Why, yes, I have a passable voice."

"Then sing now." She shuffled through some music and chose a piece. "This is a rousing number. Sing as loudly as you can." And she seated herself and began to play with great force and verve.

Meanwhile, in the ballroom Lydia approached the Marquis of Locklynde and asked, "Have you seen Miss Leonardo?"

"She was dancing the quadrille with young Tavistock when I saw her last."

Lydia frowned. "But that was some time ago. Someone

particularly wished to meet her, and I have been looking for her this age. Perhaps you could help me find her."

"Oh, I suspect she's off somewhere pinning up a flounce that was trodden on. Her partner appeared likely to do such a thing," he said off-hand.

Lydia bit her lip but did not move away to search for Esme. "You know, I haven't seen Captain Kendall for some time either."

Locklynde slanted an oblique glance at her innocent expression, then said deliberately, "If I can be of any help in finding Miss Leonardo, I will be glad to accompany you. Perhaps she is taking a bit of air on the balcony."

"Oh, I should think the night is too damp for that," she said.

"I will just look there anyway," he said, and kept her waiting for some minutes. He did not fail to notice her impatience when he returned.

He then let her guide his steps and, as they rounded a corner, came upon a most surprising scene. A small knot of people were clustered around the library door, from behind which an extremely loud voice could be heard singing a narrative ballad accompanied by an equally spirited rendition on the pianoforte.

Mrs. Milliman was standing in the forefront, red-faced with outrage. Lydia hurried forward. "What is it, Mama?"

"The most provoking thing—someone is in there playing and singing so loudly they've disturbed the card-players, and we can't get the door open or make them hear us knocking."

"That must be Esme playing," Lady Channing said, "though what she can be about I can't imagine."

"Let me knock," Locklynde said, and stepped forward to thump resoundingly on the door.

The music broke off, and after a moment a masculine voice said, "What the devil—oh, I beg pardon. The door seems to be stuck. Can someone open it from out there?"

There was no key in the lock, and pressure from Locklynde

did nothing to budge it. From the corner of his eye, he saw a very vexed-looking Lydia give a whispered order to a footman.

"If you will allow me, my lord," he said, and positioned himself in front of the door so that no one could see exactly what was happening. Locklynde, still standing nearby, was sure he had heard the rasp of a key. Then the footman flung the door open. "This door is a bit tricky, ma'am," he said to Mrs. Milliman.

Captain Kendall stood on the other side of the door. Beyond him, still seated at the pianoforte, was an unruffled Esme.

"Esme, what on earth are you thinking of? You've been disturbing the card room these past twenty minutes."

Unhurriedly, Esme rose. "Oh, I'm so sorry. Captain Kendall has such a—an interesting voice. *Molto profundo*. He thought he might be called upon to entertain later, and he wanted to practise a few songs. Someone must have been bothered by the noise and come along and closed the door. I wonder what made it stick like that?" she inquired with an innocent lift of her brows.

"Well, I hope Captain Kendall has rehearsed sufficiently because you have been making enough noise to wake the dead," her aunt said.

Mrs. Milliman was heard to murmur something about "forward girls" to Lydia, whose face was like a thundercloud.

"Come along, Esme," Locklynde said pleasantly. "I believe they are just striking up for a new set, and this one you have promised to me."

It was a country dance, and the figures drew them apart too often to allow them a sustained conversation. It was not until the set had ended that the marquis seated Esme on a sofa and said with a lift of his high-arched brows, "That was quite a performance."

She cast him a look of exasperation. "I was never so vexed.

It was that cat Lydia's work, I make no doubt. A footman summoned me to the library to attend upon my aunt, and when I arrived, there was Captain Kendall—who said he'd been given a message to meet *me*. The footman must have closed the door behind me and locked it. I could think of nothing else to do but set poor Captain Kendall to singing, for no one could think we were having a clandestine tête-à-tête while making so much noise."

His lips twitched. "No, that was hardly a love ballad he was singing."

"Poor man. He will probably be quite hoarse tomorrow. I'm glad you arrived when you did. I feared he would run out of breath at any moment."

"I believe some of the ladies had already been knocking, but you failed to hear. However, I doubt you would have been released earlier."

She directed an inquiring glance at him.

"Lydia had arranged for me to be there when you were discovered. I believe the footman had taken the key away and, on her order, was to surreptitiously unlock the door to reveal you and the captain closeted together. And since she was so very insistent that I join in the search for you, I must have been intended as chief witness to your disgraceful conduct."

"Then she must be worried that the story of our betrothal is true if she is trying to discredit me with you." Esme gave a peal of delighted laughter. "If only she knew how pointless her plotting was. As if you would care whether I was found tête-à-tête with Captain Kendall!"

"Is he a most particular friend of yours?" he inquired thoughtfully.

"Rather particular," she said. "He is so good-looking and such very pleasant company that at one time I thought it might be possible to develop a *tendre* for him. Not a serious one, of course, since as you know, I really do not have hopes to marry. But I thought it would be exceedingly romantic to have a lost love to look back on when I am old. However, to tell the truth," she confessed, "what with all my worry over luring Lydia away from Kit, I haven't really found the time to devote enough attention to falling into love."

He laughed with genuine amusement. "You feel then that it requires a good deal of attention to fall in love?"

She considered. "Well, yes, I should think so. I mean, how can one concentrate on whether one's pulse has skipped a beat or whether one feels feverish in the presence of one's lover and utterly cast down when he is away if one is always having to think of other things instead—like finding a possible claimant for Lydia's hand and keeping him interested in her and making her believe Kit will not be marquis after all?"

"Yes, I can see that such complicated plotting would take up a good deal of time," he admitted, controlling his lips with great effort.

"Well, it does," she sighed, "and I must say I never thought to spend my London Season in such a way." Her face took on a slightly aggrieved look. "And of course it is in great part your fault—but there, I mustn't rip up at you when you have been so obliging as to try to help at last. I trust that after Lydia's performance tonight, you are coming around to my viewpoint that she would not do for Kit."

"Well, the discovery that Lydia would stoop to a *scheme* has, I admit, sunk her in my esteem."

She flushed slightly and broke into reluctant laughter. "Yes, schemers are all quite odious, are they not?"

"Some more so than others," he said. And then another partner came and claimed her for a dance, and she spoke with Locklynde no more that evening.

9

ONE OF THE callers next morning at the Channing household was Lord Wittimore, who seemed anxious once again to draw Esme into private conversation. She took her cue and said, "Would you be so kind as to sit over here with me and help me wind this wool?"

When they were enough removed that the others could not hear their conversation, Esme asked, "Was there something special you wished to discuss with me?"

"It concerns Miss Milliman," he said soberly.

"She was very much in looks last night, was she not?" Esme said quite untruthfully.

He did not seem disposed to discuss Lydia's appearance but said, "She still will not allow me to speak to her father. I have wondered—I beg you will be frank with me—if perhaps your cousin could be the reason she cannot make her mind up to accept my suit."

"Drusilla?" Esme exclaimed. "Now why should Dru interfere in such a matter?"

"No, no, I meant your cousin Christopher Channing. It has seemed to me sometimes that Miss Milliman holds for him a certain regard that makes me fear for the successful culmination of my own hopes."

"Why, of course she holds him in regard," Esme said quickly. "After all, they have been neighbours since childhood. One would hardly expect her to treat an old playfellow with coldness just because she has come up to London for the

Season. Besides, Kit's uncle and Mr. Milliman are great friends. Lydia could never displease her father by being ungracious to a family friend."

"Then you do not think I need look upon your cousin as a rival?"

"Lord Wittimore, I assure you that if you are successful in your suit with Lydia, Kit will *rejoice* and be the first to wish you happy," she said fervently, glad she was able to be perfectly truthful on one point.

"You have relieved my mind, Miss Leonardo," he said. "I will just have to be patient until Miss Milliman is sure of her own heart."

"That's the spirit," Esme said bracingly.

On a drive through the park with Lord Locklynde later that day, she recounted the conversation to him. "Thank goodness he is persevering," she said, "and since Lydia's little scheme to drive us apart didn't work last night, perhaps she will think seriously about accepting Wittimore. If only she would hurry and make up her mind—"

"Why do you wish her to hurry?" he asked.

"Most especially because I fear Wittimore is desperate enough that he may not allow himself to be kept dangling forever. Then too, the sooner it is settled, the sooner Kit can offer for Verena. How dreadful if her parents should compel her to accept another suit in the meantime. Besides, as soon as Lydia accepts Wittimore, you won't have to continue to pay court to me."

"I see," he said. "You find it excessively irksome, I am sure."

"As a matter of fact, I don't," Esme confided ingenuously. "I thought I should because you do frighten one a little when you put on one of your darkling looks, and you can be monstrously high-handed. But it is surprisingly comfortable to be with someone who can always provide a glass of lemonade before one perishes of thirst and who knows which plays will be amusing and which to avoid. And I don't know anyone with whom I enjoy driving out half so much. I don't think anyone has such a pair of high-steppers as your bays or handles the reins in form as you do or wears such a stylish driving coat. And it is most amusing to watch the faces of the people we pass—some of them looking shocked because you are the wicked marquis; some of them pea green with envy over the elegance of your equipage. And to be escorted to a ball in your carriage—well, it makes me think I could become addicted to luxury very easily. It is only—''

Her voice trailed off, and he prompted, ''Only—?''

''Well, I know how sunk in boredom you must be to have to attend the sort of parties I am invited to.''

''The Milliman rout *was* insipid,'' he murmured, ''though it did have one exciting moment.''

''It makes me feel very guilty that you should have to waste so much time when I am sure you are wishing for an entirely different sort of entertainment.''

He threw her an exasperated glance, but she was looking straight ahead. After a moment, he said with a hint of amusement in his voice, ''Well, you know, Esme, dens of vice keep very late hours, and besides, I'm not invited to every insipid party you attend. *Some* of my evenings are free.''

''Yes, that's true, isn't it?'' she said, though the thought did not seem to cheer her much. Then she frowned. ''Not that it isn't your fault anyway for coming back to England at this awkward time, and for—''

''I beg you,'' he interrupted, ''don't ring any more peals over me, or I vow I shall set you down and let you walk home.''

''No, you wouldn't,'' she said confidently. ''You can be very rude when you like, but *that's* not the sort of bad manners you have.''

''You give me too much credit,'' he said. And then, in a very different voice, ''Now tell me why I found Sidney Porterfield in your aunt's drawing room this morning.''

"I scarcely see how she could have turned him away. He was only one of a dozen callers, and he is quite unexceptionable."

"I beg to differ," he said, his mouth a grim line. "And of the dozen, he was the only one at whom that foolish chit Drusilla was making calf eyes."

"Oh, surely you exaggerate," she protested, but rather faintly, as in her heart she had to agree that Dru's manner toward Mr. Porterfield was far from irreproachable. However, it would go against the grain to take the high-handed marquis's part against her own well-loved cousin, especially since when he pokered up in this uncivil manner, he put her quite out of charity with him.

"I thought I had made it clear that I do not want that relationship to continue," he stated dogmatically.

"And I thought I had made it clear that I have not the power to forbid a caller to my aunt's house."

"Esme, Esme, don't gammon me. Surely you of all people can contrive something."

She bristled. "I do not think you mean to be at all complimentary when you say that. Besides, my contriving only involves people whose affections are not engaged. If—and I do not by any means know that it is so—*if* Dru should happen to care for Mr. Porterfield, it would be outside of enough for me to interfere—and all for some whim of yours."

"You will find I am not given to whimsy," he said. "When I tell you that Porterfield will not do for Drusilla, I mean it."

With a flick of his whip, he sent his pair to a brisker trot, and they drove back to Hanover Square in silence.

The Earl and Countess of Chalfont were not among those members of society who found rakes amusing; in fact, in Kit's words, they were deucedly high in the instep. Consequently, there was no hope of Lord Locklynde's being invited to their ridotto. The members of the Channing household did receive an invitation card, however, owing to the circumstance of the countess having once, many years ago at a ball, obtained a partner for Lady Channing, or Miss Hasborough as she was then. Her own magnanimity on this occasion pleased her so much that ever afterward she was well disposed toward Lady Channing and was now happy to be able to bring pleasure to her old acquaintance by sending an invitation card.

Kit escorted them, and while his company could not fail to please, still there was something rather flat, Esme thought, in arriving at the Chalfonts' in Uncle Frederick's lumbering old coach. She wondered in passing what Lord Locklynde was doing on this evening when he was free of the obligation to do the polite to her. She certainly hoped he was enjoying himself, she told herself with unwonted vehemence.

One happy circumstance was that the Millimans were unacquainted with the Chalfonts, despite Mrs. Milliman's best efforts to effect a change in the situation, and so Kit could be perfectly comfortable tonight and spend as much time with Verena as propriety would allow.

Dru was looking adorably demure in palest pink and pearls. It was no wonder she was much sought after. There were several really nice young men who looked ready to lay their hearts at her feet if she would give them the slightest hint of encouragement. And when Esme considered that Dru saved her sweetest smiles for Sidney Porterfield, she could have shaken her cousin.

Halfway through the evening, she was watching them together, thinking it was poor taste in Mr. Porterfield to hold Dru's arm so possessively, when suddenly he bent to say something and Dru's expression became rather apprehensive for a moment. But then she nodded, and they moved toward a door. Esme quickly made up her mind to follow, not having liked the cat-in-the-cream look on the gentleman's face.

They were just disappearing down the corridor as Esme reached the door and, to her dismay, she saw them stepping outside onto the terrace. It was really too indiscreet of Dru,

Esme thought, exasperated with her cousin. She was on the point of following them when a most worthy but dull young man approached her, saying roguishly, "Ah, at last we meet when you are not surrounded by admirers, Miss Leonardo. How fortunate I am, for this time when I beg the favour of leading you out, I can feel sure you are not already engaged."

"Yes—I mean, of course I shall dance with you, but just this minute I am on an errand for my aunt. I will join you in the ballroom for the very next set." And, refusing all offers of assistance in carrying out her errand, she was at last able to persuade him to leave her, though some minutes passed before she could stem the tide of his eloquence in assuring her that she might depend upon him to do any service Lady Channing might wish.

Esme slipped out onto the terrace and at first saw no one; then, on the far side of a marble fountain, she discerned two figures standing close together. She hurried forward and, as soon as she had made certain of her cousin's identity, she called out brightly, "Oh, there you are, Dru; I have been looking for you this age. My aunt was asking for you. Shall we go back together?"

She took Dru's arm in hers and, though she felt it tremble a little, Dru followed her, saying rather unsteadily, "We just stepped out for a breath of air. It was so very warm in the ballroom."

"Yes, but you are quite cool enough now, I daresay."

Mr. Porterfield attempted no excuses but merely accompanied them in annoyed silence.

The dull young man soon came to claim Esme's hand for his promised dance, and it was perhaps fortunate that his intellect was not of a high order, for she was so preoccupied that her responses to his conversational sallies were made quite at random and could hardly have been termed sensible. Even when later partnered by several of her special friends, she found that her pleasure in the evening was quite spoilt, her only glimmer of satisfaction being derived from seeing

Kit and Verena together with happy expressions on their faces.

As soon as they were at home and had bid good night to Lady Channing, Esme went to her cousin's bedchamber. "Dru, you may tell me I have no right to sermonise, but I'm sure you don't wish to set tongues wagging. It was only by chance that it was I instead of your mama or some spiteful gossip who saw you walking alone on the dark terrace with Mr. Porterfield. I urge you to have a care."

Dru rounded on her. "You're against him, just like all the rest!"

Esme drew back, surprised. "What do you mean, I'm *against* him? I merely don't want you to be the object of careless talk."

"You *are* against him. You always were. You wanted to set Lydia onto him."

"Oh, that was just a passing thought. Actually, I find him very personable."

"But in your heart, you despise him for being poor and having to work for a living."

There were two spots of colour high on Esme's cheeks. "Drusilla Channing, how can you put such a charge to me of all people? I am poor myself. I have never despised anyone for working. My dear Cobbie works, and she is one of the best people I know! And I daresay I shall be working for a living before long."

"Oh, Esme, I'm sorry, but if you knew the slights he has had to put up with. His life has been so sad."

"Indeed? That is a surprise to hear, for his circumstances seem far from sad to me."

"Oh, but you do not know the whole. He was his mother's favourite, which made his brother hate him, and then his mother died when he was very young. He has had no one to take his part ever since. He was in the army, thinking he might make a career of it, you know. He was on General

112

Howe's staff, but all through jealousy, rumours were circulated about him, and he never got the promotion he deserved. So he sold his commission, and now his brother could quite easily make him an allowance that would help him a great deal in his effort to rise in the government, but he selfishly refuses."

"I see," Esme said soberly, and what she saw dismayed her, for she saw that Mr. Porterfield had played on Dru's sympathies and aroused all her protective instincts toward one who had been abused. But what sort of courtship was it where a gentleman talked only of the hardships he had suffered? Esme could not see that his life was so very hard. And why should his brother, who had daughters of his own to provide for, be expected to make an allowance to a man who must be nearly thirty and who had a comfortable government position? Dru had too tender a heart, that was her trouble, and Esme privately felt that any man who so openly asked for sympathy was unlikely to be deserving of it.

She kissed Dru's cheek. "We'll say no more about it, but please, Cousin, *guardatevi*! Take care!"

As she went soberly to her own chamber, she wondered what the marquis would have said had he heard Dru's comments. It would certainly not have given him a better opinion of Mr. Porterfield; she was sure of that. Guiltily, she wondered if she should tell him. She knew he disapproved of any sort of relationship between Dru and Mr. Porterfield, and she did owe him a lot for his help with Lydia, but no, she couldn't repeat something Dru had confided privately to her. Still, the whole episode gave her a very uncomfortable feeling.

It was said that the Favishams' balls were always among the best of the Season, as not only was the host enormously wealthy, but he was also willing to drop his blunt freely in order to provide his guests with every delicacy they might fancy, and his lady's cook was one of the finest in London.

Neither were the Favishams stiff, starched-up types, and accordingly their guest list always included a number of the more amusing, if slightly raffish, members of the *ton*.

Since Lord Locklynde was an old school friend of Lord Favisham, it was no surprise that he was invited, but when the invitation card for the Channings and Miss Leonardo arrived in Hanover Square, it caused a great flutter of surprise and pleasure, as Lady Channing was not personally acquainted with the Favishams and the affair was sure to be a great social highlight. She began to dither immediately over whether the girls had fine enough gloves and whether the tiny tear in Dru's pink gown could be mended invisibly.

Esme chose to wear a gown of sea green gauze over soie de Londres of the same shade, its bodice trimmed with a rouleau of silk interspersed with brilliants. She sewed some more of the diamante trim to a simple bandeau, and they sparkled like fresh dewdrops in her dark curls.

Lord Locklynde was to escort them in his carriage and had sent each of the girls a posy in a silver holder: pink roses for Dru, white for Esme.

He was looking very fine himself, Esme thought, in his well-cut black coat and white-striped waistcoat of gros des Indes. His stickpin was a simply set sapphire, but its size was prodigious.

The Favishams' house was ablaze with hundreds of candles, the staircase so crowded that Esme thought the evening would be half-over before they reached the top. It was by far the largest ball she had attended, and she could not help being a little glad for Lord Locklynde's presence in guiding her and Dru through the crowd as she feared she would have felt lost indeed without him.

By the time she had reached the ballroom, she had met several of her friends and had the gratification of having a number of dances bespoken. She did not know quite how, but Locklynde had managed to lead both of them to Lord Bartling, who immediately claimed Dru's first dance and supper as well. Before Dru could answer, Locklynde had spoken for her. "Capital. Then the two of you can join Miss Leonardo and me."

Dru looked around rather helplessly as if hoping, Esme thought, to claim a prior invitation from Mr. Porterfield, but as he was nowhere in evidence, she murmured her acceptance in a low tone, which Esme hoped Lord Bartling attributed to shyness rather than sulkiness.

Once out on the ballroom floor, she was caught up in the excitement of the gala affair, but as the evening progressed and it became more and more crowded, she was glad of the chance to escape for a few moments and went down a corridor, hoping for a breath of air.

She thought she felt a refreshing draught, as if a window were open somewhere, and was following it when she saw Lord Locklynde coming out of a side room deep in a low-toned conversation with a distinguished-looking gentleman. Just as she was almost opposite them, the other man said, "Thursday at three, then," and took his leave of the marquis.

He turned and, seeing Esme, said, "You are no doubt seeking some air. It is a squeeze in the ballroom, is it not?"

"Yes, it is," Esme said, frowning a little. "Lord Locklynde, that gentleman you were speaking to—I'm sure I have met him, but I can't think where."

"I shouldn't think it likely. He doesn't go out in society much. His name is Sir Wilfred Kenner, and he has a position in—" he paused—"in the government."

She felt he had intended to be more specific than to say merely "the government" but had stopped himself. "His name is not familiar to me, but I'm sure I have seen him somewhere," she persisted, "though it doesn't seem to me it was at a social occasion."

He seated her on a sofa in a sparsely populated side room where the air was cool, left, and reappeared in no time with a glass of lemonade. Just as she took the glass, it came to her, and she said impulsively, "I know where I saw Sir Wilfred. It was in Hyde Park on a side lane, in conversation with Miss Wild."

Her companion stiffened, and suddenly she realised it was a gaffe to have mentioned Theodosia Wild to *him*. She gave a tiny gasp of dismay and then bent her head to her glass so that he could not see her face.

"You are acquainted with Miss Wild?" There was an odd note in his voice.

"No, not acquainted, but Dru pointed her out to me. She is so very striking that one could not mistake her again."

"I did not know that Dru was acquainted with Miss Wild," he said implacably.

She gulped but thought she might as well be open about it. His *affaires* were no concern of hers, after all. What was it to her if Miss Wild had been his inamorata—or still was, for that matter—unless it would come to Lydia's ears, of course. "Well, Dru is not acquainted with her either, but she saw her with you at the theatre once, and her cousins explained who she was."

"I see." She could not tell if his tone held amusement or annoyance. For some reason, the situation was making her feel very gauche, as if she were no more than a schoolroom miss. Not enjoying the sensation, she stiffened her spine and gave a very creditable little laugh. "Good heavens, Locklynde, you can hardly suppose that I consider your relationship with Miss Wild to be of any interest to me!"

"No indeed. How could you?" he said blandly, which made her wish to hit him.

Having decided that the fresh air had restored her quite enough, she rose and said she believed she would go back to the ballroom.

Supper was a lavish spread and somehow, though Esme had determined to partake lightly and with utmost sophistication, Lord Locklynde had supplied her plate with the very choice delicacies that she most liked so that she ended by clearing her plate and even accepting a second helping of marrons, though of course it may have been that she was merely preoccupied in helping Lord Bartling to entertain Dru. While the two gentlemen had gone to fetch refreshments for the ladies, Dru had said to Esme with feigned nonchalance, "In such a squeeze, it's difficult to meet all of one's friends. For instance, I have not even caught a glimpse of Captain Kendall or Mr. Porterfield."

"I danced a country set with Captain Kendall, but I haven't seen Mr. Porterfield either. Perhaps he was not invited or had another engagement."

Dru seemed so cast down that Esme felt compelled to behave with utmost vivacity and soon, between them, she and Lord Bartling had Dru laughing, and the supper party ended up very merrily with Esme hardly giving any thought at all to whether Lord Locklynde was still caught in the toils of the dashing Theodosia Wild.

=10=

THE NEXT DAY, all three of the Channing girls, their mama, and Esme had forgathered for a simple luncheon: nothing more than cold meats, some cheese, a bowl of fruit, and bread and butter. As they were nearly finished and Esme sat peeling a peach, Lady Channing picked up a letter that had been brought in by the butler, read it and, with a startled exclamation, dropped it as if it had been a snake. "Heavens above us!"

"What is it, Mama?" Hope asked.

Her mother frowned at the missive. "It's a great mark of condescension, of course—but all the same—however, if Honoria is there! Well, it isn't as if we would meet any Cyprians or that sort of thing, but still—though if he is ever to do anything of consequence for Kit—and of course now with Esme—oh, I do wish your Uncle Frederick had not returned to Wellspring House this very week and could tell me what I ought to do!"

"The first thing you must do is tell us what you're talking about, Mama," Dru said firmly.

Her mother raised the sheet of heavy notepaper and waved it feebly before her. "Your cousin—Locklynde, that is to say—has invited us all—even Hope and Constance—to visit the hall."

"Locklynde Hall?" Connie gasped.

"What other hall would he be apt to invite us to?" her

mother said, speaking sharply, more from nerves than irritation. "He has never done such a thing before, and of course it is a magnificent place, quite worth seeing, as I well remember from having visited there when your poor father was alive, but with your cousin's reputation—and the parties they do say he used to give during those brief times he was back in the country—I hardly know what Frederick would say. Though he does mention that it is to be a very small party and that Honoria will be there to serve as hostess, and *she* is perfectly respectable; of that I am sure."

"Mama, you are acting like a pea-goose," Hope said pertly. "I hardly think my cousin could be so foolish as to invite you to accompany us to his family seat if he had anything but the most proper entertainment in mind. It does not seem to me that his brain could be so disordered."

Hope's bracing words seemed to have a good effect on her mother. "Oh, I am sure you are right. After all, he has been the soul of propriety in accompanying us to balls these past weeks, to say nothing of his comfortable carriage. He has never said anything beyond the line—has he?" she appealed to Esme.

"No indeed, aunt. He has been all courtesy." Esme's brain had been working furiously, and she knew she must bend every effort to convince her aunt to accept the invitation, for when Lydia found out that she was visiting Locklynde Hall, it must go a good way toward convincing her that matters between Locklynde and herself were indeed serious.

Kit came into the room then, and the invitation had to be laid before him. After hearing the whole, he seconded Hope's opinion that his mother was a great gudgeon if she imagined there would be any havey-cavey goings-on with her invited along as chaperone.

"And who is Honoria?" Esme wanted to know.

"She is Jared's elder sister. The Lady Honoria Whitechappel. She was widowed several years ago."

"You never mentioned he had a sister," Esme said to her cousins.

"Oh, well, in explaining bloodlines, females don't count," Hope said wisely.

"I think it will be splendid," Connie said.

Esme was inclined to agree, but she could not help noticing that Dru was maintaining a morose silence. Could it be that she would wish to forego a visit to a great country estate because she knew Mr. Porterfield would not be among the guests? If so, her feelings for him must be more serious than Esme could comfortably contemplate.

Kit, on the other hand, had divided feelings. He would hate to miss even for a few days the tantalizing glimpses he was allowed of his beloved Verena. However, it would be a considerable relief not to have to walk the fine line between mere courtesy to Lydia and an actual declaration. On the whole, he thought he would like to go. There was bound to be some sport at Locklynde Hall and, a countryman at heart, he was beginning to chafe in the confines of town life.

"If only Frederick were here," Lady Channing mourned, but rather feebly this time, as if her mind were already made up.

"Now, Mama," her son said, "what could Uncle Frederick possibly say that is to the point? You know the girls will be safe enough with both of us to look after them. And since I'm Locklynde's heir, it would look deuced odd if we didn't accept the invitation."

"I suppose you are right," his mother said. "Well, girls, we must look to your wardrobes."

As the marquis had specified that it was to be a small, informal party, they agreed that no ball gowns would be needed—only a few evening dresses for the older girls, morning dresses, and their riding habits.

Esme was pleased that she had just finished remaking for herself a white mull round-gown and had daringly trimmed it with knots of coquelicot. Now she needed only some wide coquelicot ribbons for her leghorn gypsy hat and she would feel fine as five pence.

The marquis had gone down to the hall earlier and had kindly left his own carriage to convey the ladies, with Kit riding alongside. Lady Channing took great comfort in this circumstance, as it meant that she was not left with the worry of writing to her brother to ask if he would object to their taking his conveyance. She did write to him of their visit, but rather cravenly, or so she felt, left it until too late for him to object. Esme would have called it prudent instead.

Even at the clipping speed of some ten miles an hour, the journey was a lengthy one and left Esme a great deal of time for reflection. Now that the flurry of preparation was over, she had the leisure to wonder exactly what had prompted the marquis's invitation. Was it possible that he had simply become so bored with squiring her to balls that he had decided that having her down at Locklynde Hall would serve the purpose as far as Lydia was concerned, and yet at very little trouble to himself because, once down in the country, he could ignore her if he chose. He might spend his time riding off with the excuse of looking to his acres or engaging in some sport as gentlemen of property could always do, thus leaving her entertainment to his sister's charge. Well, if that was his idea, it was certainly all right with Esme. *She* had no interest, save in convincing Lydia that it was useless to hope that Kit would one day inherit the title. This manoeuvre should help to further that interest. Still, she could not think that being seen in her company at a few balls should have been so very onerous a burden to Locklynde that he needed to bustle the whole family out of town in order to be free of it. But then she knew very little of what went on in the marquis's head. Sometimes she thought she had caught a glimpse of humour that appealed to her own, but often his face was a mask, giving nothing away. Perhaps he really had found the time he spent with her hateful. She bit her lip. If that was the way he felt, she would take good care to keep out of his way and make no demands on his time down at the hall.

After half an hour or so of such lowering conjecture, her lips curved in spite of herself as she recalled the firm way in which the marquis had handled Lydia when she had hinted so odiously for an invitation for herself. Locklynde had been driving her in the park when they had come abreast of Lydia's phaeton, and she had waved them to a stop.

"I thought I must say good-bye, Esme, since Kit tells me you are all going down to the country."

"How kind of you. Good-bye, Lydia."

"Will you miss the Terwilligers' ball next week? It would be a shame. I hear there is to be an Eastern theme, with hundreds of ells of paisley making a giant tent of the ballroom."

"The time for the family's return has not been definitely set as yet," the marquis had said pleasantly.

"I almost envy you your journey," Lydia had said plaintively. "The weather is unseasonably warm, and the multitude of social engagements has become quite fatiguing. A sojourn in the fresh country air would renew one's spirits, I am sure."

"We can by no means count on that, Miss Milliman. The Cotswold country is apt to be sultry at this time of year. I cannot recommend its air as salubrious, but my sister never comes up to London anymore and has expressed a wish to see her cousins and to meet Miss Leonardo. But we must not keep your horses standing. Good day." And with a bow to Lydia, he had set his own pair in motion down the path.

Esme came out of her reverie to look out the windows of the carriage. They were passing through one of the dense beech forests of the Chiltern Hills, and the light filtering through the trees enveloped all she could see in a luminous golden glow. Her aunt was dozing in one corner. Hope and

Constance were whispering together so as not to awaken her; Dru was staring straight ahead at nothing, her mouth drooping a little in discontent. Esme had worried, so uninterested had Dru been in preparing for this journey, but now that they were actually on the way, Esme hoped her cousin would cheer up in reaction to the novelty of the situation when they reached Locklynde Hall. Meanwhile, Esme determined to thrust all cares from her and enjoy the sights of the countryside.

Beyond the Chilterns, they entered the Vale of Aylesbury. They stopped for tea at the post house in the village of Aylesbury, which Esme found charmingly quaint with its narrow alleys of Tudor houses, so different from anything she was accustomed to.

They continued northward into Cotswold country with its rich flat meadows, rolling wolds, and gentle streams, where village and farm houses were all built of the local grey limestone. As they wound their way still further north where the Cotswolds met the ironstone hills, the buildings took on a honey-coloured tint.

At last Lady Channing said that if memory did not fail her, she believed they would soon be able to see Locklynde Hall. Esme thrust her head out of the window and gasped as the carriage turned up a wide beech avenue at least a mile long, at the end of which stood an imposing manor house of creamy stone, golden in the slanting rays of the late afternoon sun.

The carriage swept around a circular reflecting pond and deposited them at the graceful porticoed entrance. A footman in crimson livery handed the ladies down, and they were ushered by the butler into a marble entrance hall where the marquis came forward on unhurried steps to greet them. At his side stood a tall lady, somewhat older than he, with hair as dark as his save for a few streaks of white.

She greeted Lady Channing with a kiss, they each declared

mendaciously that the other had not changed a whit, and then Lady Channing presented her offspring, "though I believe you did see them once, at least the older two, when they were hardly more than babes. And this is my niece, Esme Leonardo, my late sister's child."

Lady Honoria took Esme's hand in a firm grasp. "I hope you will enjoy your stay, all of you. And now I'm sure you must be dropping with fatigue. If you wish to go up and wash away the stains of travel, I will have the maids bring tea to your rooms, and perhaps you can lie down upon your beds for half an hour before dinner."

A footman showed Esme to a charming bedchamber, its walls covered in claret-coloured toile paper. The fabric of the bed hangings matched the paper, and a stuffed armchair was upholstered in a claret-and-cream stripe. A maid was already unpacking her things, and a hip bath stood filled before the crackling fire. Almost immediately there was a knock, and another maid brought in a tea tray.

The tea and the bath revived Esme so much that she had no need to lie down, but immediately completed her toilette and risked going downstairs by herself in hopes of finding someone to talk to.

The butler materialised at the foot of the steps and directed her to the green drawing room. This was of impressive size, some thirty by sixty feet, almost all windows on the north and west sides, their swagged brocade draperies now drawn. A Siennese marble fireplace in the south wall had a cheerful blaze, and on one of the settees flanking it sat the marquis and his sister.

Esme hesitated, as they seemed deep in conversation, but Locklynde caught sight of her and rose at once, taking her by the hand and leading her to sit by the Lady Honoria. "You will find us sadly dull at dinner tonight, I fear," she told Esme, "but perhaps after your journey you won't mind that. Tomorrow a few other guests will arrive: a very pleasant relative of mine and her two daughters who are near to your own age. She is a cousin on my late husband's side of the family, the Whitechappels, you know—as of course Jared has alienated most of the Channings, and one scarcely knows which of them to ask if one doesn't wish for an uncomfortable visit."

Her brother merely cast her a quizzical glance and a reproachful half smile.

"Then I have invited several young men down from town to keep Kit amused: Sir Edwin Childress, Jack Catchpole, and Lord Bartling."

Esme lifted her brows delicately and turned to her host. "Are you sure it isn't Dru whom you are hoping will be amused by Lord Bartling?" He looked nettled but, before he could make an irritable retort, she went on, "I like him very well myself and think he would make a splendid *parti* for Dru, but I wonder why you think she will let you choose for her?"

She could see he was annoyed, but he kept his voice even. "Your imagination is too vivid, Esme. I don't give a farthing whether she takes Bartling or not, but I believe he is a friend of Kit's and one whom it will do Dru no harm to associate with."

At that moment the others of the party entered the room, and after a little general conversation, dinner was announced.

A breakfast tray was brought to Esme's room next morning, and after she had eaten and put on a sprig muslin gown, she opened her door but did not hear any sounds of life. So, having neglected to discover which rooms belonged to her cousins, she went downstairs.

Still finding no one, she thought she would venture out of doors and, discovering a French door that opened directly onto the lawn, she stepped outside and was just enjoying some invigourating breaths of morning air when a smart little gig clattered around from the other side of the house and Lady Honoria jumped out and threw the reins to a groom.

"I was hoping to arrive before anyone was down," she greeted Esme.

"Arrive?" Esme asked, puzzled. "But don't you live here?"

"No, I live in the dower house half a mile away—not that Jared wouldn't like to install me here. But it's too large for one woman, and he is away so much. My son and his wife have also urged me to make my home with them, but to tell the truth, my daughter-in-law and I rub along together much better when we see each other for no more than two or three weeks at a time. Besides, I have a passionate interest in the gardens here, and Jared indulges me by giving me free reign. I'm afraid they were rather neglected during my father's later years, and though Jared is willing enough, he's seldom here. His head gardener is a wonder, but I have my own ideas I like to see carried out, so being here suits me very well."

"I shall be delighted to go exploring," Esme said. "Your English gardens are so different from what I'm accustomed to."

"Well, we do have one Italian garden which was made to accommodate some statuary my grandfather brought back from his Grand Tour. He planted a circular yew hedge with niches for the statues and a fountain in the center. The yews have grown up tremendously since then and I'm afraid are rather overwhelming the statues, but they are second-rate and not in very good condition anyway, and I can't bear to have the yews cut back. I suppose I should go in now in case your aunt is up and about, but perhaps you would like to see the gardens a little later."

"Oh yes, please. I'd like that very much."

They went in to find Lady Channing in the morning room, eager for a comfortable cose with Honoria, catching up on family news. Fortunately for Esme, Lord Locklynde came in just then and invited her for a ride. She and her cousins had not brought their horses down from London, but her host assured her of a suitable mount, so she ran upstairs and quickly donned her riding habit.

Down at the stables, a pretty little mare was brought out for her. "She has high spirits," the marquis told her, "but no bad habits. I think you'll get along well together."

"I'm astonished that you should think so," she said, smiling ruefully, "since you believe me to be a creature of so many bad habits myself."

"I'm sure I never said so uncharitable a thing," he protested. "I might merely have dropped a hint that telling rappers and trying to run other people's lives were not altogether suitable occupations for a lady."

"But I'm always very relieved when I *can* tell the truth—without its interfering with my plans—as it is so much more comfortable," she said.

He laughed, and then the groom put her up on her mount and they were away across the fields. After a lively gallop, they slowed their horses and cantered easily along together.

"Oh, this is glorious!" Esme cried. "I love this countryside. It is so tame always to be riding in the park."

"You may ride whenever you like as long as you're here."

"Thank you for coming with me this morning, but you won't have to again now that I know the way. I'm sure you have more important things to do."

"Well, since I brought you all down here to entertain you, I can think of nothing more important than doing so."

She flushed. "You don't have to pretend, my lord. I know how irksome it must have been for you in London, always having to hang on my sleeve. It was a very good plan to invite us down as it is nearly sure to have a good effect on Lydia. I would not be at all surprised to find she has accepted Wittimore by the time we return to London."

He threw her an exasperated glance. "Do you think it

might be possible for you to forget about Lydia and her tiresome affairs for a little while? I realise you've appointed yourself guardian angel of your cousin Kit, but you might try letting him pull his own chestnuts out of the fire for a bit.''

"The way you are doing with Dru,'' she flashed.

His mouth hardened. "That, my child, is quite another matter.''

How quickly his mood could change, she thought, shivering a little. Sometimes he was charming; she could even be quite easy with him when he was merely ironical, but his dark looks had the power to put a sharp thrust of fear into her.

When she returned from her ride, she went exploring the house, as all she had really seen of it beyond her own bed-chamber were the green drawing room, the entrance hall, and the dining hall. Now in daylight, the curtains in the drawing room were open, and she was charmed to discover that the windows gave directly onto the lawn, where she could see giant Lebanon cedars, and off in the distance the shimmer of a lake bisected with a graceful arched bridge.

The house had been built in the 1750s on the site of an older one that had been pulled down, according to Lady Honoria, and was arranged for comfort, unlike some more ancient dwellings that had been added to piecemeal, according to their various owners' whims.

One thing that particularly impressed Esme was the art-work displayed. There was a particularly fine Grecian head on a pedestal in the hall and a malachite table in the drawing room that was a treasure. Of course, the walls had their share of indifferent portraits of earlier generations of Channings, but most of the paintings were of real quality. She went from room to room, finding none that were not appointed with the most exquisite objects, but the paintings especially amazed her. There were Veroneses and Titians and Cara-vaggios and a whole collection of the Flemish and Dutch schools, including a breathtaking Vermeer and a van Eyck.

In a sunny morning parlour, she was just studying a small Italian painting by an artist with whose name she was not familiar when Honoria came into the room. Suddenly Esme gasped, "But this must be quite new! I know that villa, and the small pavilion that shows in the picture was built only a few years ago."

"Yes, my brother sent it home about six months ago," Lady Honoria said. "In fact, almost all the pictures in this room are fairly recent acquisitions."

Esme blinked. "Lord Locklynde bought these paintings?"

"Yes, and a good deal else here in the house. Our father was not at all interested in art, and most of what my grandfather acquired was distinctly second-rate. You see, the original Locklynde Hall was badly damaged in a fire, and very few of the furnishings were worth saving. When the new house was built, the idea seemed to be to fill up the walls as quickly as possible, but the mediocrity of the pictures always offended Jared."

"But this is a magnificent collection," Esme said in a bewildered way.

"Yes, I believe so. Jared looks to the interior of the house while I bend my efforts to the gardens."

"But it must have taken a great deal of time to find all these things and acquire them."

"Well, as you know, my brother has spent most of the past years abroad."

"Yes, but—" Esme began and then clamped her mouth resolutely shut. She could hardly say to his sister that she wondered how he had found the time for his collection between chasing his ladybirds and frequenting gambling casinos. It showed a rather new dimension to the marquis. Her cousins had said he was prodigiously lucky at the tables, but it took more than a mere fortune to assemble a collection as fine as this. It took effort, and it took taste. Somehow she had not pictured the wicked marquis as a serious art connoisseur. And yet the evidence was here before her eyes.

"Would you like to see one of the gardens now?" Lady Honoria asked, and Esme immediately expressed her pleasure.

They went out the east door of the house and found themselves on a broad terrace with steps leading down to a formal garden. Stone urns on pedestals flanked the top of the stairway. The beds were laid out in curving geometric shapes, and the colours shaded into one another so delicately that Esme was enchanted. Lavender spikes of catmint were surrounded by pink roses, and the scent was heady. "Oh, it is so fragrant," she cried.

"Yes, that is from the tuberoses and mignonette and heliotrope," Lady Honoria said. "These Parson's Pink China roses, which are my special pride, also have a lovely aroma."

They walked among the beds, Esme's delight all that her companion could wish, until a footman came to inform Lady Honoria that Mrs. Dunreith and her daughters had arrived.

"Come and meet them," she said, linking her arm with Esme's, and they went into the drawing room where the guests were waiting.

"Sophronia, how good to see you. And Alicia, how pretty you are. Emily, you're grown as tall as your sister. Esme, come and meet my cousins: Mrs. Dunreith, Miss Dunreith, and Miss Emily Dunreith; Miss Leonardo."

Presently all four of the Channing ladies came in, and introductions were made all over again, after which Lady Honoria rang for tea. Esme studied the newcomers. Mrs. Dunreith was of medium height and pleasantly plump, probably closer to fifty than forty, with a good-natured expression. The two girls looked to be within a year or so of each other in age, both with red-gold curling hair, but Emily, who favoured her mother in looks, seemed the more placid, while her elder sister was extremely vivacious.

Before dinnertime, the three young men the marquis had invited down from London had arrived so, since Hope and

Constance were allowed to dine with their elders, they were fourteen at table.

The food was not overly elaborate, but there was a great variety of dishes, all superbly prepared, and it occurred to Esme to wonder how the cook's time was spent all those months when Locklynde was abroad. Of course, there were the servants to feed. Did he employ this many footmen and maids all the year round even when he was not at home?

Across the table, Lord Bartling was seated between Dru and Alicia Dunreith, but Dru was so languid that Esme wanted to shake her, and Alicia, chattering away volubly, claimed most of his attention. Esme's own dinner partners were her cousin Kit and Jack Catchpole, both of whose conversation she always enjoyed, so she passed a very pleasant meal.

=11=

THE NEXT MORNING, Miss Dunreith pounced upon Esme when she was no more than down the stairs and suggested a walk in the shrubbery. Esme was not averse to a walk at such an early hour, but Miss Dunreith had such an air of intensity about her that she hoped she was not going to be made privy to some awful secret she would rather not hear. However, Miss Emily was also there, looking at Esme with what she imagined to be a rather anxious look, so she agreed.

They were no sooner out of the house than Miss Dunreith said, "You must call me Alicia and I will call you Esme. Is that all right? I want us to be great friends."

"I hope we shall be," Esme said politely, though inwardly doubtful about the matter.

"Now you must tell me all about Locklynde."

Esme was a little taken aback at the avidity of her tone. "You mean Locklynde Hall? I am not very well acquainted with it yet, having arrived only the day before yesterday. It can boast some exquisite pieces of art, however."

Alicia gave a shrill laugh. "Not Locklynde Hall—Lord Locklynde, the marquis."

"Why, what do you want to know?"

"Anything that would be useful."

Now Esme felt puzzled. "Useful in what way?"

"Oh, don't play the innocent," Alicia said. "Has he declared the reason for this house party?"

Esme shook her head, but her new friend persisted, "It

must be obvious. He is getting on in years and feels it is time he takes a wife. He has invited us down here to make his choice from among us.''

Esme gasped. "I think you mistake the matter!"

"No, don't you see? With his reputation, he can't afford to be too nice in his distinctions. We and the Channings are family connections whose mamas he has not quarrelled with, so he could count on our coming. He could scarcely ask some stranger to bring her daughters to Locklynde Hall—not a respectable stranger. I knew at once what was in the wind when the letter from Lady Honoria arrived because he has never invited us here before. Emily has no interest in bettering herself." She gave her sister a rather scornful glance. "We both have beaux at home, and she is quite content with hers, but I determined at once that I would like the marquis, no matter what sort of man he was. However, that will not be as hard as I feared because he is really not at all ill-looking except for those eyes of his, which are a bit scarifying.''

Esme was in a turmoil of emotions, principally indignation at the presumption of this brass-faced girl, but even while one part of her mind was taken up with deciding how best to depress Alicia's pretensions, another part was thinking that she was quite wrong about Lord Locklynde's eyes, which, while they could pierce one in a scarifying fashion, could also light with humour and intelligence. In fact, Esme now perceived that they were quite his best feature.

"I saw at once that Constance was too young, and I presume you are also out of the running, being a foreigner.''

Esme was speechless.

"Alicia, your tongue is running away with you," her sister said in a mortified tone.

"Oh, Esme must see that if Locklynde wanted a foreign wife, he would not have come back to England to do it. What he needs is a wife with some proper background to bring him a measure of respectability.''

Esme's mouth had dropped open in outrage, and she

closed it with an angry snap lest she descend to exchanging insults with this brazen creature.

"So, as I see it, the race is between Hope and Drusilla and me. Hope is a little young, of course, but he might think her all the more malleable for that. Now, as you have known him up in London, tell me, what sort of girl does he like?"

"I do not believe I have ever heard him express a preference," Esme said stiffly.

"Well, we know what his *preferences* are, but I'm sure he is looking for something different in a wife. The question is, does he want a quiet wife who will stay in the background and let him do as he pleases, or one who will run his home in a fashionable way and be a notable hostess?"

"And which sort would you be?" Esme asked in a faint voice.

"Oh, I am very versatile. I can be whichever he wishes."

"The way you are running on," Emily said, "no one would think you could be a quiet wife."

"I'm sorry I can't help you," Esme said. "Truthfully, I believe you have mistaken the reason for this house party."

"Well, even if that were so," Alicia said with a toss of her bright curls, "it is far too good an opportunity to pass up. I do not care a fig that he is a rake, and I would take a more ill-favoured man by far in order to be mistress of all this."

"Take care, Alicia," Emily said with a worried frown. "You will have Esme believing you are a good deal too coming."

The warning came far too late. Esme already did.

Esme had intended to ride that morning, but she found herself so angry she went to her bedchamber to compose herself instead. "Of all the encroaching—" She bit back a most unsuitable Italian word and paced about the room. She would have liked to take Alicia Dunreith by her copper curls and— No, this was no way to calm herself. She sat down in a chair by the window and tried to let the sight of the broad lawns and feathery cedars sink into her consciousness.

For whatever reason Locklynde had gotten up this house party, it was not to choose a wife among Hope, Dru, and the Dunreith girls—of that she was sure. She had thought perhaps he was tired of her company and sought to bury her in the country for a while so he could attend to his own pursuits, but so far he had been an attentive host, taking her riding and offering to do so again, and he had promised to attend the al fresco luncheon his sister had planned for this afternoon. No, that could not have been his only reason for bringing them here.

He did not seem like a man who acted from whim. There must be a reason, but what was it? Could it be Dru? Not that he would assemble a group to choose from among—that was foolish, for he had an entrée to many of the great houses of London, and plenty of more likely prospects than that odious Alicia Dunreith—but could it be that he was interested in Dru and, seeing that she had developed a *tendre* for Sidney Porterfield, he had thought to separate her from him by this ruse?

He was certainly unreasonable about Mr. Porterfield. Could it be jealousy? The thought made her very agitated, and she jumped up and began pacing again, though it certainly shouldn't have agitated her, for her own visit here would serve very well to discourage Lydia, and that was Esme's only goal, wasn't it? But somehow the thought was like a pin come undone and jabbing one at a time when one could not stop to remove it. And then she decided she had found the answer. Dru did not care for her cousin Jared at all. She disapproved of him wholeheartedly and hadn't even wanted to come down to Locklynde Hall. That was why the thought of Dru and the marquis had upset her so. She wouldn't want Dru to be unhappy, and of course if Locklynde offered for her, she might feel bound to accept for

Kit's sake—as well as for all she could do for her mama and sisters if she were the Marchioness of Locklynde.

But the whole notion was foolish beyond anything, for if he were the least bit interested in Dru, then why was he throwing Lord Bartling at her head?

Deciding there was nothing at all to support the notion that Locklynde had a romantic interest in Dru, she felt very much better—for Dru's sake of course—and began to dress her hair for the afternoon outing.

As the day was fine and crisp rather than sultry, she chose a round dress of soft rose jaconet muslin with long sleeves and a frill of lace at the throat, surmounted by a short embroidered pelerine of deeper rose gros de Naples.

In addition to the guests staying at the hall, Lady Honoria had invited several neighbouring families. The spot chosen for the luncheon was a summerhouse beside the lake a half mile from the main hall. Because of the distance, a variety of conveyances had been brought around from the stableyard for anyone who wished to ride. With the older people comfortably settled in the more commodious vehicles, Hope and Constance delightedly claimed a pony cart, saying they hadn't ridden in one for years.

Esme and Dru declared their intention of walking, as did Emily Dunreith, the young men of the party, and some of the neighbours. Lord Locklynde, holding the reins of a spruce little gig, asked if anyone else would like to be driven, whereupon Alicia vowed that she would hate to ruin her new kid slippers and drew her skirts aside to reveal her blue-shod feet, along with rather more ankle than Esme thought necessary.

Lord Locklynde jumped down and helped her into the gig, then handed his sister up beside her and said, "You will want to arrive early and see to the arrangements, Honoria. I will walk with the others." As the gig set off, Esme was delighted to observe the expression of fulminating irritation Alicia cast backward at the walking party.

They made up a very merry group, everyone in such high spirits that even Dru laughed and bantered with the rest.

As they rounded a curve in the path, Esme stopped dead-still, and her breath caught in her throat at the sight of the pillared, domed summerhouse on the far side of the lake. Locklynde was at her side in an instant. "Is anything amiss?"

"Oh no," she said, and to her embarrassment felt tears pricking behind her eyelids. "It's just so very lovely. It looks from here as if it were floating in the water."

"Yes, I have had that same thought," he said quietly.

"It should be painted," she said, "to capture it forever. What a charming picture it makes, all the shades of green contrasted, the silver willows and the pale beeches and the Lebanon cedars almost black, all reflected in the lake. And the terraced orangery sloping up behind with its brighter colours. Did your sister plant that?"

"Yes; she has a touch of genius, I think. I believe she would have made a very good professional landscape gardener if she had been a man."

"It must give her great pleasure to be able to do as she likes here."

"I hope so, for she is the best there is," he said. "Shall we cross the bridge now and join the others?"

Servants had earlier brought tables and chairs and laid out the banquet, as well as setting up an iron ring at the end of an alleyway in the grassy lawn for a game of Pall Mall. On the center table, there was every sort of meat and game pie, galantines and aspics, tender asparagus, poached salmon, and quantities of fresh fruit piled high on salvers.

Several sizeable tables were set under the domed roof of the summerhouse, but some of the smaller tables and chairs had been placed on the lawn. Esme chose a spot near the water's edge and had a delightful time throwing bits of roll to a family of snowy ducks afloat on the lake.

After the lengthy repast, some of the young men went rowing on the lake while others of the party engaged in a spirited game of Pall Mall. "Did you know this game in Italy?" Jack Catchpole inquired of Esme.

"Yes, but we called it *pale maile*," Esme said. "I only tried it once, and my shots went so wild I never did get the ball through the ring."

She watched the game for a while and then noticed that Lord Locklynde was seated sketching. She went over and stood beside him. "May I look, or does it make you nervous to have someone watching?"

"It doesn't make me nervous, but I'm afraid I haven't done justice to my subjects."

"Well, it would be difficult to do justice to any view in this setting, for whatever subject you choose must be surpassingly beautiful."

"Yes, I agree, and perhaps that is my problem," he said and handed her several sheets from his sketch pad. There was one of the arched bridge, others of the flowery terrace, and one was a chiaroscuro of the trees around the lake. "They are quite worthless," he said and made as if to crumple them.

Without knowing she intended it, she caught his wrist, surprised at his taut strength. "Oh no, please, may I have one—as a souvenir of this day?"

His wrist stilled under her hand, and suddenly she let it go.

"Choose any you like. This is the only one I shall keep." She looked on his pad then and saw that it was a sketch of herself beside the lake, tossing crumbs into the water for the ducks.

Hardly knowing what she did, she chose one of the sketches quite at random and, murmuring a confused thank you, retreated. It was so warm, she thought. She should have taken off her pelerine. It had made her quite hot and breathless.

The next day, an expedition had been planned to visit a

nearby ruined abbey, which everyone enjoyed almost as much as the lavish tea at a charming inn on the way back.

Alicia Dunreith, having managed to insinuate herself into Lord Locklynde's carriage, was in a very good humour, tossing her curls and posing affectedly in various decayed archways, taking an apparently great interest in abbey life. "And what, pray, might this be, Lord Locklynde?" she asked, pointing dramatically to a heap of loose grey stone.

"Why, Miss Dunreith, that is a pile of rocks," he answered solemnly, sending Constance into a spasm of giggles.

The day afterward, Esme expressed her intent to ride, and by the time she arrived at the stables, she found Locklynde there, as well as Alicia and Sir Edwin. Alicia's habit was of blue velvet with a matching hat trimmed with three curled ostrich plumes.

The two girls were mounted first and, as the groom brought out the horses for the men, the scene seemed to explode. Later Esme was to play it back in her mind. Everything was quite normal, the girls' mounts dancing around in eagerness to be off; then Alicia put up her hand as if to adjust her hat. Her hand came down, and suddenly her mare gave a wild snort and stood straight up on her hind legs, pawing at the air. Alicia slid off her back shrieking and, as the frenzied creature came down, one forehoof struck Esme's mare on the flank.

Startled by the sudden blow, the mare bolted. Esme had not had a very good grip on the reins and, by the time she remedied the situation, the frightened beast was too far out of control for her to be able to stop the mad flight. They were running straight across a field, and Esme was torn between her fear of being thrown and her fear that the mare would step in a hole and break a leg. The wild ride seemed to go on forever. Esme's breath was coming in great sobs of exhaustion and fright. She was managing to keep her seat but did not have the strength to slow her mount.

And then suddenly she heard hoofbeats behind her, pulling up beside her, and there was Locklynde on his huge stallion, urging him a little to the fore of the mare and close beside her so that the marquis could reach the mare's bridle with one strong hand.

As the stallion slowed, the mare's pace was forced to match it until at last, with heaving flanks, the poor creature stopped. Locklynde was off his horse in an instant, ready to catch Esme as she tumbled trembling from the saddle.

She slid down into the protection of his arms, and they closed about her. She thought she had never felt so safe in her life. She stood there, her breath coming raggedly, her head against his chest, and she could hear the hard beating of his heart. In that moment, she had a sudden blinding revelation as to why she had so disliked Alicia Dunreith and why the suggestion that the marquis was trying to choose a wife between Alicia and Dru had made her so uncomfortable.

She looked up at him then, the tears sparkling on her eyelashes blurring everything a little, but she could see his dark eyes: not frightening now, but full of concern for her.

"Esme!" he said. "Are you all right, child?"

She nodded but still leaned against the strength of him.

Then she heard more hoofbeats and a voice behind her, and stepped out of his arms.

It was one of the grooms mounted on a grey hack and leading another mare.

"Everything's all right, Jenkins," his master said. And to Esme, "Do you think you can ride back? I'll be beside you all the way."

"Oh yes," she said, and they helped her to mount the fresh mare.

"Bring Molly back and rub her down," Locklynde said to the groom, and they made their way slowly home.

In the stableyard, a groom was still stroking Princess and

leading her up and down. Kit had appeared and looked relieved to find Esme was in one piece.

"How did you happen to be such a clunch as to let your horse bolt with you?" he demanded.

"She took me by surprise," Esme said lightly, "but it wasn't her fault."

"Is Miss Dunreith intact?" Locklynde inquired.

"I think so, but she's mad as fire. Seems to think you had no business galloping off instead of rescuing her. Very put out about it. We carried her into the house, shrieking fit to kill. Claims her ankle is broken, but Emily says it isn't even swollen, so that seems unlikely. They've sent for the bonesetter though, and she vows she'll be laid up here for days."

Locklynde grimaced. "Well, that is Honoria's problem as we shall return to London on schedule." Of the groom he asked, "Is Princess all right?"

"Yes, my lord. She's calmed down nicely. No damage, except there's a spot of blood on her neck. I don't see how she could have gotten it." Then he held something out to his master. "I found this gold pin on the ground. It looks to be valuable. Mayhap the lady dropped it when she fell." His eyes met those of the marquis blandly.

"Yes, no doubt," he returned in an ironic tone. "I'll see that it is returned to her."

Up in her bedchamber, Esme took off her riding habit and stared at herself in the mirror hanging over the serpentine dressing chest. Her hair was dishevelled, and there was a smudge on her cheek, but that wasn't what bothered her. There was a new look about her mouth, a new expression in her eyes. Where was the face of the self-confident, self-sufficient, practical-minded girl who had always looked back at her out of the mirror? This was the face of a woman in love. It had a softer look, but an anxious one. She caught at her berry red underlip.

It was all so impossible. She dared not let Jared see how she felt, and with a start realised that it was the first time she had called him Jared in her thoughts. He had been so quick to believe, way back at the beginning, that she was trying to get Lydia out of the way so she could have Kit for herself. How much worse—how humiliatingly worse if he should come to believe she had told Lydia the lie about their engagement in order to entrap *him* in some way. But he couldn't think that, surely. She hadn't even met him then. There was no way she could have known he would turn up. But might he think that once the situation had arisen, she had taken advantage of it?

She covered her face with her hands. She couldn't bear to be another Alicia—plotting to ensnare him. She couldn't bear to have *him* think it of her either. She would have to tell him that she had decided he was right. If Lydia had not already decided to give Kit up in favour of Lord Wittimore, she would stop interfering and let Kit pull his own chestnuts out of the fire as Jared had suggested.

But that would mean Esme would have no excuse to see the marquis anymore. And how could she bear that? It was all such a tangle. She had never meant to fall in love with anyone, and she wished now that she hadn't. No, she didn't. It was terrible, but it was wonderful too.

Was there the slightest chance that he cared just a little for her?

It seemed incredible, but the way he had held her and the look in his eyes before the groom interrupted— Perhaps it was her imagination. She remembered the luncheon by the lake when he was sketching and had implied that all the views he had taken were beautiful, and there had been one of her—the only one he had kept.

She pressed her hands to her cheeks, and they felt flaming to her touch. She walked over to the writing table and picked up the sketch she had chosen, remembering the feel of his wrist under her hand. She ran her fingers over the paper, studied every line he had drawn, and at last put it away in a drawer under her best gauze scarf. It had been an exhausting morning. She decided she would lie down upon her bed and rest.

The next day was the last before they would return to London. After a light luncheon, everyone disappeared—some to take a last walk about the grounds; Lady Honoria to go to the dower house and attend to a few matters, she said; the older ladies to doze. Esme tried to be helpful in offering to read to Alicia who, though the doctor had given her a clean bill of health, was stubbornly lying upon a couch in the morning room, wearing some sort of pale pink drapery which not only fought with the colour of her hair but was singularly inappropriate for that time of day. The invalid rejected Esme's offer with a look of malice.

"I wonder you dare speak to me after what you did yesterday," she said, "letting your horse run away with you just to make yourself interesting."

Esme opened her mouth to give Miss Dunreith a piece of her mind, decided it wasn't worth it, and withdrew from the room.

She wandered about, looking at everything for the last time: the paintings, the views from the windows, each aspect showing a different side of the Locklynde lands and each lovelier than the last. She was standing at a north window when she saw Jared coming back down the path that led to the dower house. It reminded her that Lady Honoria had invited her to come and see her kitchen garden and herbararium, and she had not yet done so. Catching up a wide-brimmed straw hat, she set off down the path.

Some fifteen minutes later, she went through the gate of the dower house grounds and saw someone walking across the lawn toward a little arbour. Her first thought was that she had never seen Honoria looking so smart. Her dress was a striking black and white stripe with a black spencer. Then she heard Honoria's voice from the other side of the lawn saying,

"Esme, my dear, I'm so glad you came," and at the same moment the figure in black and white turned and, to Esme's stupefied shock, she saw it was Theodosia Wild.

She stood rooted to the spot as the colour drained from her face. She felt as if she had turned to stone. She wanted to run away and hide—no, she wanted to die. But then Honoria had drawn Esme's hand through her arm and was leading her forward. "Esme, this is Miss Wild, who has come to pay me a little visit; Theo, this is Miss Leonardo."

Theodosia Wild looked down from her statuesque height and said in a rich, full voice, "I'm happy to meet you, Miss Leonardo. I had the pleasure of hearing your father sing on several occasions. You must have been very proud of him."

Esme stammered some reply—she was never sure what—and then Honoria was guiding her to a walled garden and saying, "Esme has come to see my kitchen garden." Blindly, Esme looked where her hostess was pointing—at the delicate herb beds; the chive gone to flower, waving purple heads; the neat rows of vegetables ringed all round with marigolds and lobelia; the espaliered trees against the honey-coloured stone wall—but she did not know what she was seeing.

She thought it would never end, but at last Honoria was offering her lemonade, and she was saying in a voice held as steady as she could manage that she must return to the hall.

She walked back up the path until she was out of sight of the dower house, and then she fled into the woods, sheltered herself behind a pine with low-hanging branches, and fell to the ground weeping.

Jared's mistress *here!* And staying with his sister! Had she been here all along? Was that why he had come down to the country? But surely he could have seen her as easily in London. He had come from the dower house a little while ago. All the other times when he had not been visible at the hall—had he been visiting Theo Wild? Did Honoria know what she was? Surely not, for Aunt Dora had said she was very respectable. But why was Miss Wild staying at the dower house? Esme could hardly credit that Honoria would have knowingly arranged for her brother to hold assignations under her own roof.

The Wicked Marquis. That's what she had called him in her mind, and then he had lulled her with a promise to help in her plan to save Kit from Lydia, and though she knew he had some purpose of his own for doing so, and though she had been a little frightened of him, she had accepted his help. And gradually, under his clever handling, her fears had dissipated and she had come to think him a man of taste and charm, and she had discounted the stories she had heard about him. And only yesterday, she had fancied herself in love with him. He had become Jared to her, but now her eyes were open and he was the wicked marquis again.

At last she rose and brushed the leaves from her dress, wiped the tears from her cheeks, and crept back to the hall. Once in her room, she removed the sketch the marquis had made from under her scarf and tore it into a thousand shreds.

She should have heeded Papa's advice. It was all very well to make well-intentioned plots but not when one fell a victim of one's own strategy. Papa had cautioned: Never light a fire you can't quench. She had lit a blaze that had flamed too high, too brightly, and she was the one who had gotten burned.

Later Esme never knew how she had managed to get through that last dreadful night. She smiled until her face ached, spoke without knowing what she said, and when she was asked to play the pianoforte, she was glad to escape into the music, where she did not have to look at anyone or think of anything but the notes.

Blessedly, because of tomorrow's journey, they made an early evening of it, and Esme entered her little red and white bedchamber for the last time and lay down under the toile canopy to a restless and miserable night.

She made her thank yous the next morning without ever looking directly at the marquis, even when he took her hand

and wished her a safe journey. She was so exhausted from her sleepless night that she managed to doze off in the carriage, having thought as she closed her eyes that she wished the journey would never end and that the coach would drive forever until they fell off the edge of the world into oblivion.

= 12 =

A NIGHT'S SLEEP in her room in the house in Hanover Square did a certain amount, if not actually to revive her spirits, at least to stiffen Esme's spine, and it was with a semblance of her old liveliness that she went down to the breakfast parlour. There she found her aunt sorting through a stack of invitation cards.

"Well, Esme," she announced, "we can be busy every day of the week if we choose. You girls are having quite a social success, I should say."

"In my case, Aunt, it is all owing to your good offices in my behalf."

"Nonsense. It is your own charming manners. And of course, being seen so often on the arm of a marquis hasn't hurt either, for though many people disapprove of him, all the stories about him do pique people's interest, and they are bound to be curious about any young lady of quality who can capture his attention."

Esme winced but remained silent. Was that what Locklynde thought, that she had sought his escort to advance her own social pretensions? Well, let him think it. His opinion could never matter to her again.

"Now, the Marshfields' ridotto is this very evening. Shall we accept?" her aunt was saying.

"Why not?" Esme shrugged. At least Locklynde was not expected back in London for another day so she would not have to meet him there.

In fact, one of the first people she saw at the Marshfields' was Lord Wittimore, and his glum expression made her heart sink. She made her way across the room to him and held out her hand. "Well, we meet again, my lord. Have you any good news to tell me?"

He shook his head. "I fear I have not."

"You and Miss Milliman have not quarrelled, I hope?"

"Oh no, how could I quarrel with anyone so—so perfect?" he said through clenched teeth. "Sometimes I dare to hope she returns my feelings, but she will not commit herself."

"Maidenly modesty is said to be a virtue," Esme counselled. "She is shy. Don't be of faint heart. *Coraggio!*"

"There are times when I think I am wasting my time." Then Esme saw that his eyes had alighted on a Miss Duffield who, though she had no personal beauty—indeed, a pasty complexion and bulging, vacuous eyes—was dressed in the height of fashion and wearing a huge emerald pendant and matching eardrops. She could almost see Wittimore speculating as to how badly her father would like to get her off his hands.

"Ah, you are admiring Miss Duffield, I see. And no wonder. She is all that is amiable, poor girl. I believe she has a hard time of it. Her father has ruined several eligible *partis* for her, I believe, for though he is extremely well to pass himself, he insists on an enormous marriage settlement before he will bestow her hand," she improvised. "And yet she is so good-natured she never complains."

With relief, she saw that his interest in Miss Duffield had abruptly waned.

Feeling exhausted and depressed after her latest invention, Esme moved on, almost ready to give the whole thing up. But then she caught sight of Verena, her lovely face turned up to Kit's with her heart in her eyes, and she knew she must still try her best.

She could not feel guilty about spoiling Miss Duffield's

chances with Lord Wittimore. Her father's money could doubtless buy her any number of husbands, and Wittimore was not exactly a bargain

The next evening was an assembly at Almack's. Lord Locklynde, who had arrived in town only that afternoon, looked in very late. When he sought Esme out, she informed him coolly that all her dances were bespoken already.

Something flickered in his dark eyes, but he only said, "That is my loss," and went away again very soon. Esme congratulated herself on brushing through the meeting with so little emotion, but she felt rather numb afterward and was . glad when her aunt collected her to go home.

The next morning was so fresh and lovely that she decided on a ride in the park and went downstairs to see if one of her cousins would like to accompany her. In the hallway, she saw Dru sorting through the letters that had been delivered and snatching one up, slipping it into her pocket. "Dru, would you like to ride with me this morning?" Esme asked.

Dru jumped and turned with a guilty expression. "What? Oh no, I can't. That is, I must go to my room and mend the hem of my white sarcenet gown." She turned and fled up the stairs as Esme watched with a frown. It was a very transparent lie, as Dru never touched a needle if she could help it, and her mama's maid did all of her mending.

Eventually, Hope and Constance decided they would ride with her, but a fastening on Hope's riding habit had come loose, and Esme had to repair it for her, so it was some time before they entered the park.

They met various friends, several of whom joined their party, thus slowing their progress until Esme declared that Peaseblossom was itching for a little more strenuous exercise than dawdling along in this leisurely way and that she would turn down a side path that she had on past experience found usually to be deserted and catch them up later.

She let Peaseblossom into a decorous canter, wishing she were in the country back at Wellspring House and could ride at breakneck speed. Suddenly, in a small clearing in the shrubs off to the right, she saw two figures standing very close together, one in a blue dress just the shade that Dru had been wearing this morning. Hardly able to credit what she saw, she recognised that it *was* Dru with Sidney Porterfield, her hands clasped in his.

She wheeled her mare and turned back up the path. This was very bad. Dru had no business having an assignation in the park, and it could be nothing else, as there was no abigail nearby and Dru had said she had to stay home and mend her dress. Was the letter she had so furtively slipped into her pocket from him, naming the meeting place and time? She could only suppose so.

As she rode slowly back to the others, her mind was in conflict. Lord Locklynde had been very particular that Dru not become entangled with Porterfield. He had seemed to think she had some influence with Dru, but she didn't. She had cautioned her, but Dru had chosen to ignore her warnings.

She didn't know what to do. It would upset her aunt too greatly to hear such news; Kit had been unexpectedly called to Tydings this morning; and even if her Uncle Frederick had returned to London from Wellspring House, she would not go to *him* with such a tale.

At one time in the not-so-distant past, she would have informed Dru's cousin Jared and let him deal with the matter as he thought best, but she would not, *could* not go to him now. He was the last person in the world to moralise to Dru—he who had established his mistress in his sister's house, practically under the noses of his aunt and cousins.

He had put himself beyond the pale and had no right to serve as anyone's conscience. She would not go to *him*. There was nothing else for it—she would have to confront Dru herself.

She steeled herself to it that afternoon, going to Dru's bedchamber, where she was changing her clothes.

"Oh, Esme, you startled me," she said. "I am rather in a hurry just now, as I have some shopping to do."

"I must talk to you, Dru. Quite by accident, I saw you with Mr. Porterfield this morning," Esme said abruptly.

Dru's brush clattered to the floor. After a long moment, she turned. "Have you told Mama?"

"No, for it would upset her greatly, as you very well know, if she discovered you had been meeting a man in the park alone. How did you come to do such a—an indecorous thing?"

Dru turned and paced about the room silently, her hands pressed tightly together.

"If you are going to continue to behave so shabbily, I will have to tell my aunt," Esme said, "for no matter how much it will distress her, it will be worse to have your reputation in shreds."

"No!" Dru cried suddenly. "You must not! Indeed, there is no need for—for we were saying good-bye." Her cheeks, pale before, were now very flushed. "He was so very unhappy that I had to meet him. You see—you see, he wrote to Uncle Frederick some little time before we left for Locklynde Hall to ask permission to pay his addresses to me. My uncle didn't even do him the courtesy of replying. It is just one more slight to a man who has already endured many—and all because he has no fortune. As if I cared for that!"

"That is very noble, Dru, but I don't see that he suffers so many slights. He has a responsible government post, and he is received everywhere."

"Not everywhere," Dru flashed. "You will notice my cousin Jared did not include him in the house party at Locklynde Hall."

"Well, it is true that he does not seem to care much for Mr. Porterfield, but—"

"And it is all jealousy that has held him down."

"Jealousy?" Esme was astonished. "What possible reason

151

would your cousin have for being jealous of Mr. Porter-field?"

"Oh, I don't know that *he* is particularly, but Sidney's brother is, and it was jealousy that kept him from advancing in the army."

"How?" Esme asked skeptically.

"Oh, because he was so popular with the men below him, you know, and some of his superiors didn't like that because they were unable to inspire the same kind of loyalty. And then there was a most unfortunate incident—the sort of thing that does happen to a man of his address. He was in no way at fault, but the wife of one of the officers conceived a totally unreciprocated *tendre* for him and was foolish enough to let it be seen."

For a moment, Esme was silent. She sensed that Dru would not care to hear any remark she might make on such a tale. At last she said, "I do not see why any of this should make it necessary for you to have an assignation with him."

"But don't you see? After my uncle's insult, there is only one thing we can do, and that is to—to part. Would you like to bid good-bye to someone you cared for under the noses of a drawing room full of guests?"

"And now you really have put an end to it?"

Dru turned her face away and said in a small, choked voice, "Tomorrow begins a fresh page."

Esme went away feeling extremely uncharitable toward Sidney Porterfield. Any man who would make such a display of his vast collection of slights and injustices was a poor creature indeed. How Dru could have been taken in by him she could hardly credit. But then, she reflected, she had so little sensibility herself. Perhaps she had been born without it, or perhaps she had needed to put it aside in order to survive. She could not fault Dru for her tender heart. Her cousin had obviously been attracted to Mr. Porterfield from the beginning, as sometimes people were for no discernable reason, and afterward, instead of his odious whining filling her with disgust, it had aroused her sympathies.

Well, though it was very bad of Dru to have had a secret rendezvous, she was not the only one in her family to be taken in by the wrong man. Even Esme herself had, just for a brief span of hours, fancied she had given away her heart, and only think what a mistake that was.

They went to the play that night with several of Lady Channing's older cronies. Dru had dressed in a white gown she had vowed several weeks ago that she was so tired of she never wanted to see again, but tonight she seemed too abstracted to care how she looked. From her seat, Esme caught sight of Lord Locklynde in Sally Jersey's box with a group of others she did not know. Resolutely, she kept her eyes on the stage.

During the first interval, one of her aunt's friends, Mrs. Downing, asked Dru to accompany her while she walked about a bit. Shortly afterward, she did not so much hear someone enter their box as sense a new presence. She looked up to see Lord Locklynde had entered. He was looking as elegant as ever in his evening dress, but she gave him the briefest of glances before dropping her eyes.

He chatted pleasantly with her aunt and her aunt's friends, but as Esme was sitting with several people between the two of them, he had no chance of private word with her. If he had wanted one. She thought he tried to engage her eye, but at this distance she could not be sure—did not want to be sure.

Finally he made his good-byes and went away again. As he turned to leave, Esme held her hand up as if to stop him—to tell him she needed to talk to him—that she was worried about Dru. But no, he was not one to judge Dru's actions. She let her hand fall. Besides, she thought, Dru had assured her that all was over between her and Sidney Porterfield. "Tomorrow begins a fresh page," she had said. Esme wondered if she quite believed her. She had at the time, but now, as she sat in the dark box, she recalled again Dru's reddened cheeks and the way she had not met her cousin's eyes. If only Kit were here. She found she could not concentrate on the play. Instead, her mind returned again and again to her conversation with Dru.

At the second interval, she looked toward Lady Jersey's box, but it was now empty, and none of its recent occupants returned for the rest of the evening. They had probably gone on to some party. So if she had wanted now to tell Lord Locklynde about Dru, she had missed her chance.

When they arrived home, Dru retired to her own room after kissing her mother tenderly but barely uttering a brief good night to her cousin.

Esme slept badly and awoke hardly later than the birds. Of course, it had been an early night last night, not like staying out dancing halfway till dawn. It seemed too early to get up, but she could not slip back into sleep either. Perhaps it was the coolness between herself and Dru that was making her so miserable. Dru had scarcely spoken to her all evening. In a way, it was understandable. Dru must have been unhappy enough yesterday at having to part from Mr. Porterfield without being scolded by Esme, who was after all only her cousin, not her guardian.

She wished she could think of some way to make amends. She smiled. It was a frivolous thought, but perhaps it would let Dru know she was sorry. She got out of bed and found her favourite parasol, French lace with roses, which Dru so admired. She scribbled a little note that said, "Forgive me." She would creep into Dru's room and leave the note and the parasol on her dressing table, where she would see them immediately she awoke.

Out in the corridor, she could hear the clatter of baking pans in the kitchen below, but no one was stirring abovestairs. She gave a tiny scratch at the door in case Dru should be awake and, when there was no answer, she quietly opened the door and slipped in. Tiptoeing to the dressing table, she started to lay the parasol down when she saw there was a letter propped up against the mirror which said "Mama" on the outside.

With a terrible sense of foreboding, she whirled around. Dru's bed was empty. She pulled open the window curtains and let light stream into the room, then jerked open the wardrobe doors and saw that a good many of Dru's clothes were missing.

The little lace parasol dropped unheeded to the carpet as she snatched up the letter. Hesitating only for an agonising moment, she unfolded it. There were several blots upon the words, as if Dru had shed tears over it.

Dearest Mama, it said. *I know you will be distressed, but please don't be too angry. I am doing the only thing I can by going away with Mr. Porterfield. If only Uncle Frederick had given his consent for Sidney to pay his addresses to me, it would all have been different, but it is hopeless. This is the only way. He has a special license, and he is taking me to his family home because even though his brother is disagreeable, Sidney thinks it will help to lessen the scandal if we are married from there. I only wish you knew him better and you would understand. He has been so often and so unjustly maligned—I cannot bear to break his heart.*

If you can, forgive your loving daughter
                                        Drusilla

Esme gave a little groan of despair. "What am I to do?" She covered her face with both hands. She was very much to blame. If *only* she had warned Jared how serious Dru was about Sidney Porterfield. If only she had swallowed her pride and not let the fact that Theo Wild had been at Locklynde Hall keep her from telling him about Dru's assignation in the park. She should never have so gullible as to believe they were saying good-bye. Perhaps in one part of her mind, she had never believed it but only wished to.

If she could reach Kit—but by the time she had sent a message to Tydings it would be far too late. There was only one person she could turn to, and that was Locklynde. Her feelings toward him could not be taken into account at such a moment, and whatever his personal life might be, she never doubted that he could somehow set things right.

She took the letter back to her own room and thrust it into a drawer. Ringing for the maid, she began to dress quickly in a walking costume. When the little maid came to the door, she had Esme's breakfast tray. "You're up early, Miss."

"Yes, Betty; if Lady Channing should ask, tell her Miss Drusilla and I have both had breakfast and gone out. And tell Roskins to bring the carriage around as quickly as possible."

Betty gave a little bob and went out, her expression puzzled.

Esme swallowed half a roll and a few sips of coffee, and then adjusted her bonnet. Fortunately, her aunt always slept late, breakfasted in her room, and wrote a few letters before venturing downstairs. That would give her a little time before an alarm was raised.

The elderly coachman gave her a reproachful look. He knew something havey-cavey was afoot with Miss Esme ordering the carriage at this ungodly hour. If only the master was here, he would report it to him.

"Take me to Lord Locklynde's house," Esme ordered.

Worse and worse, Roskins thought. Visiting a gentleman's house alone and at such an hour. It wasn't fitting. Foreign, that's what it was. He wished he had the rumgumption to say no to Miss Esme, but her expression didn't bode well for anyone who crossed her.

She gave an imperious ring at Lord Locklynde's door. It was opened after some delay by a butler who had a very annoyed look, which turned to consternation when he saw a young lady standing on the doorstep.

"Kindly tell Lord Locklynde that Miss Leonardo wishes to see him at once on a matter of great urgency."

It was on his tongue to tell her that he wouldn't wake his lordship at this hour for a royal duke, but something in the young lady's face made him think he might do so after all if it were within his power.

"I'm sorry, Miss, but his lordship is not at home."

She knew he must be shocked at her arrival alone at a gentleman's house, but she could not concern herself with such considerations now. "I know this is an awkward hour, but if you will give him the message, I'm sure he will see me."

"I'm sorry, but when I said 'not at home,' I did not mean not at home to visitors. I meant that his lordship is away from home."

"But he can't be," Esme cried. "Where is he?"

"I wouldn't know, Miss, his not having confided his destination to me."

"But I saw him at the play only last night. Where could he have gone so early this morning?"

The butler's expression was disapproving, but he said, "He did not leave this morning. He left very late last night, taking with him a small portmanteau."

"But don't you have any idea where he has gone?" she persisted, unable to believe that he would not be there when she needed him so desperately.

"No, Miss, I would not," he said firmly.

Reluctantly, she retraced her steps to the carriage. What was she to do? She had no idea how to set about recovering the runaways. She had counted so much on finding Locklynde. He was Dru's cousin and the head of the Channing family. And besides, he was the sort of person one could turn to with confidence of his knowing what to do. She *had* to find him, but where? She bit her lip.

There was only one person she could think of who might

know. But if it had been difficult to humble herself by coming to Lord Locklynde's house, her next stop would be a thousand times worse. Still, she could not see any other way.

"Roskins, do you know the Montgrove house in Belgrave Square? Please take me there at once."

He shook his head to himself over Miss Esme's strange ways, but set off and at last pulled up in front of a square Palladian mansion. "Here we are, Miss."

She leaned forward. "And which is the Bookertons' house?"

He indicated one two doors down.

"Then stop in front of the one between them."

He feared for Miss Esme's sanity. He really did. Foreigners!

The butler who opened the door gave the merest flicker of surprise at seeing her before his expression returned to one of imperturbable neutrality.

"Please apologise to Miss Wild for the earliness of the hour, but tell her that Esme Leonardo *begs* a few moments of her time. It—it is of the utmost urgency."

For a fraction of an instant he hesitated, and she feared he would turn her away, but then he led her to a little satin-covered chair and told her to wait.

The minutes seemed to stretch out, and then there was a rustle of taffeta and she looked up to see Theodosia Wild in a sort of dressing robe of black watered moiré with a frill high up around her throat, her skin incredibly white above it.

"Miss Leonardo," she said in her pleasant, rich voice. "I hope you will forgive my deshabille, but Benton said it was urgent."

Esme swallowed. "Please, Miss Wild. I most urgently need to speak to Lord Locklynde "

There was a little surprise on Miss Wild's face now. "You thought he might be here? I assure you he is not. I have no idea where he is."

Esme studied her face. "You would not say that just to—I assure you nothing of that sort matters now. I just didn't know where else to turn. You're certain you can't think where he might be?''

"No, I can't." Miss Wild frowned a little. "It seems to me you must have a serious problem. Could you tell me about it?''

Esme shook her head. "I'm afraid it is nothing you could help with.''

"Perhaps I might. You never know.''

Afterward, Esme was not sure why she had confided in Theo Wild. In fact, it seemed almost incredible to her that she had done so. Miss Wild was the last person she had ever wished to see again. She was, as Dru had said long ago, an unsuitable person to know. And yet Jared cared for her, and his sister seemed to be her friend. Perhaps it was Miss Wild's air of calm confidence that loosened Esme's tongue, or perhaps it was a look of compassion in her eyes. She swallowed hard and then blurted, "My cousin Drusilla has run away with Mr. Porterfield. Mr. Sidney Porterfield." She was completely unprepared for Miss Wild's reaction.

"My God, she must be stopped," she said with astonishing vehemence. "She will ruin herself! Tell me everything you know.''

Esme blinked a little at Miss Wild's passionate outcry. "I happened to go into her room very early this morning. Her bed was empty, and there was a letter directed to my aunt, Dru's mama that is, on her dressing table. I opened her wardrobe and saw that some of her clothes were missing, so I—I opened the letter.''

"Quite right," Miss Wild said. "What did it say?''

"She said that since her uncle refused his consent, there was no way but to elope with Mr. Porterfield. She had told me earlier that Mr. Porterfield wrote to her uncle at Wellspring House some time ago asking permission to address her.'' She hesitated and said a trifle uncomfortably, "I don't know how much you know about the family. Wellspring House is the country home of Dru's uncle and mine,

Frederick Hasborough. At any rate, he told Dru that her uncle had insulted him by not even deigning to answer the letter.''

"Hmmm.'' Miss Wild's fine, dark eyebrows arched skeptically.

"Dru told me that they had decided they couldn't see each other again, but in the letter she told her mama they are eloping. She said he has a special license and is taking her to his family home to try to help minimise the scandal. His brother's seat is in Derbyshire.''

"Yes, I know. And she is underage. Porterfield and his brother don't get along. I believe the brother to be an upright man. I doubt he would lend his countenance to any such action as a runaway marriage. Porterfield will probably make for Gretna Green.''

"You do think he plans to marry her?''

"Oh yes, of that I am sure,'' she said grimly. "And that mustn't be allowed to happen.''

"But—''

"Never mind. Speed is essential.'' She opened a door and beckoned to her butler. "Benton, have Davis bring around the four-in-hand at once. I want three outriders.'' He disappeared without a blink, and she said to Esme, "Does your aunt know of this?''

Esme shook her head. "Not yet.''

"Do you have any engagements for this evening?''

"No. Yes—oh, it is so hard to concentrate. Yes, a ball, the Merrimans' ball.''

"That will be such a squeeze that, with luck, you won't be missed. And if you are, your aunt can contrive some ailment. Here is pen and paper. Write to her and tell her that Dru has run away but that on no account is she to raise an alarm. Tell her you are going after Dru and will see that she comes to no harm. Your coachman can deliver the note when he returns the carriage.''

160

Esme had barely had time to finish the letter before a servant entered the room dressed in a brown travelling cloak and plain bonnet that shaded her face. In a deferential voice, she asked, "Are you ready, Miss?"

"Yes, whenever Miss Wild—" she began and then stopped and stared in disbelief at the nondescript figure before her. "*Miss Wild?*"

There was a hint of laughter in the voice. "Yes, it is I." She took the note from Esme, folded it, and affixed a seal. "As soon as the portmanteaux are loaded, we can go."

"But I don't understand."

"Well, a young lady like you can hardly set out on a journey without an abigail. And, though I hope for the best, we can by no means be confident of overtaking them in time to return to London tonight. I do not plan to save your cousin only to raise a scandal concerning you. Locklynde would have my skin for it. In fact, I probably shouldn't even take you, except that you may be able to handle your cousin better than I, once we have her back. Come now."

Esme's head was swimming. Nothing Miss Wild said made any sense to her, but she seemed intent upon rescuing Dru, so what was there to do but follow?

Miss Wild's light travelling carriage was comfortable and built for speed. "We head north," she said. "Whether he takes her to Derbyshire or to Gretna Green, it is the road he will follow. What time did you last see your cousin yesterday?"

"When we arrived home last night from the play, it was not quite midnight."

"And there were still servants up, I presume?"

"Yes. A footman to answer the door, my aunt's dresser, and one maid to help Dru and me."

"She could not have left then until the house was settled for the night. And the mail coaches leave at night. Since Porterfield has his own dray, I assume he would not take her on the stage but would travel post. Let us hope she crept out early this morning, only a few hours before us. And if you wish to pray, then pray I am right.''

"I shall," Esme said in a conscience-stricken voice, "for I fear I am much to blame.''

"You? How?''

"Lord Locklynde told me from the beginning that he didn't want Dru associating with Mr. Porterfield. I—I thought he was being high-handed and dictatorial. I did try to hint Dru away from him because I thought him unworthy of her but—but I did not try any schemes to part them, as the marquis thought I should be able to do. I should have tried harder. And then, after we returned to London from Locklynde Hall, I knew she met him in the park illicitly and by appointment, but when I taxed her with it, she told me she was telling him good-bye forever. I shouldn't have let her gammon me. I should have told Lord Locklynde.''

"And why didn't you?''

Esme was silent. How could she tell Miss Wild it was because she was so jealous and disillusioned that she had hardened her heart against him?

"Well, never mind," Miss Wild said after a penetrating glance at Esme's face. "I don't see how she can have been such a gudgeon as to run off in this stupid way.''

"He played on her sympathies until she saw him as a tragic figure. But I'm sure she was genuinely attracted to him at first—one of those unaccountable things, though of course he *is* personable. And then yesterday, when he told her that Uncle Frederick hadn't even paid him the courtesy of an answer to his petition, she saw it as all of a piece with the other slights he's suffered.''

"She's a worse nodcock than I thought. I will lay you odds he never wrote to her uncle at all. He wouldn't dare, for if he had, it would surely have come to Locklynde's ears, and he would have put a stop to it. But letting her believe that her uncle had ignored his application, and there was no hope but to run away together—yes, that was clever, I'll give him that. But I do not think much of her judgement."

"I suppose where the heart is involved, one is not always wise," Esme said in a muffled tone.

"Well, perhaps Locklynde was unwise too in not being more open with you about Porterfield, but it was a matter for discretion, and he did not know you very well at first."

"I do not believe I understand you, but if there was a question of discretion involved, Lord Locklynde had little reason to trust me, Miss Wild," Esme confessed.

"If I am to pass for your abigail, I think you must accustom yourself to calling me either just Wild, or Theo."

Esme smiled suddenly at her companion, who had so unaccountably become her ally. "Thank you, Theo. And I wish you will call me Esme."

"Only when we are private," Theo said, smiling back.

= 13 =

AT BARNET, THE yard of the posting house was large and crowded and so busy and noisy with cries of "Horses up!" that Theo said, "We shall waste no time asking after them here. They should be well beyond this point, and no one in this place is likely to remember them."

In two minutes, the booted and spurred post boys in their yellow jackets and curly beaver hats were ready, the horses were changed, and they were on their way again.

"I do not see how we shall ever hope to overtake them," Esme mourned.

"We shall have to hope that they will not be travelling as fast as we shall be. At what time would your cousin have expected her note to her mother to be discovered?"

"Not until mid-morning or later. The maid never goes into her room until Dru rings. And my aunt breakfasts in bed and then answers her letters, so she would not have been looking for Dru earlier."

"And when your aunt did read Dru's note, what would she have done?"

"Oh dear," Esme said ruefully. "I'm afraid she would have fallen into spasms and then wished my Uncle Frederick were there to tell her what to do."

Theo Wild gave her an understanding look with a hint of amusement in it. "And Dru would know that. In fact, she was probably counting on its being some time before anyone decided upon any logical course of action. So you see, they will not realise the need for speed. She can have had no breakfast, so they will surely stop to eat on the way. We will not, as I have brought a hamper of food along, and my coachman has been instructed to spring the horses wherever possible."

At each post stage when the post boys were paid off and new ones took their places along with a fresh team, one of Theo Wild's outriders made a brief inquiry and reported to her. At the fourth stage, she turned triumphantly to Esme. "They stopped here to eat. We are a good deal less than two hours behind them."

"Oh, but how can you be sure it was they and not some other lady and gentleman?"

Theo gave her a repressive glance. "My man knows Porterfield's dray and can describe it accurately. At a posting house, people might not be carefully observed, but a carriage would be. Come, let us have something to eat now. This news should have revived your appetite. I'm afraid it is very simple fare as there was no time to have anything elaborate prepared."

Though Esme had earlier refused even to think of eating, the sight of the food now awakened her appetite. The hamper contained loaves of bread, cheeses, and a variety of fruits. "This is feast enough," Esme said, gratefully accepting a chunk of bread and a piece of cheese.

Her hunger assuaged, she sat peeling an orange and thinking that this was surely the strangest and most unlikely day of her life. To be hurtling through the countryside in an incredible alliance with Theodosia Wild, of all people, enjoying a nuncheon!

The mad flight continued and the afternoon was fading, along with Esme's spirits, when they pulled into the courtyard of a posting inn, and by the time the horses were changed, Theo's man appeared at the coach window to say, "The gentleman is having a pint and ordering supper. The lady is in a private parlour."

"Thank God," Theo said. "Now quickly. Go to the lady and tell her that you have a message from Mr. Porterfield. Tell her that he says he fears they have been trailed and recognised and that he has thus arranged for a change of carriage to throw their pursuers off the track. She is to accompany you at once without attracting any attention to herself and get into the new carriage. Bring her here and help her into this coach before she has a chance to speak to Porterfield or see us."

Esme almost held her breath and, though not more than three or four minutes passed, it seemed a lifetime before the door opened and a white-faced Dru was half-hurtled into the carriage.

The coachman started his team at once, and Dru was flung into a seat. As her startled eyes became accustomed to the dimness inside and she recognised Esme, she gasped, horrified, "Oh no! You must let me out at once! Esme, how could you?"

"How could you, Dru? You know it was very wrong of you."

"I do not need to answer for my actions to you!"

"No, but what do you think your mama would say if she were here, or Kit, or Uncle Frederick?"

Dru's face took on a mulish look, and she peered at Miss Wild. "Who is this? She is not from our household."

"For the moment, I am serving as Miss Leonardo's abigail, and yours," Theo said in a calm voice.

"You look familiar. Oh, what does it matter? You must take me back at once. Poor Sidney. What will he think? He must be frantic when he discovers I am gone."

"Yes, I imagine he may be, but it may take him some time to search the inn and its environs. By the time he is on the road again, I trust he will not know where we have gone, as we turned off the main road a little way back," Theo said.

"I will not go anywhere with you. You must put me down

at once!" Dru looked as if she would climb out of the carriage, but as it was rattling along at a spanking pace, that was obviously not possible. She burst into tears. "You have ruined everything!"

Esme let her cry herself out, offering only a clean handkerchief, which Dru flung back at her, fumbling in her reticule for one of her own.

With a final hiccup, she turned accusing eyes upon Esme. "I never thought you would be such a beast."

"It is not beastly to save you from a terrible mistake," Theo Wild said.

"I do not see that it is any of *your* business," Dru said, and turning to Esme, "It is not a mistake. Sidney loves me. And—and what do we care for the opinion of the world? Society has dealt so unkindly with him already that a little more scandal-broth means nothing to him. He will risk all to be with me."

"But scandal has not yet touched you, Dru. If he truly loved you, he would not let it."

"He does love me, and we would have been pleased to wait and marry in the ordinary way if Uncle Frederick had not ignored his request to pay his addresses to me. So there is no other way but to elope."

Esme had at once seen the force of Theo's opinion that Sidney Porterfield had never written to their uncle at all. "If you had waited to talk to your uncle, things might have been very different," she said to her cousin. "Neither your mama nor your Uncle Frederick is pressing any other suit upon you. Why could you not take time to talk them around? Your mama allows Mr. Porterfield to call at our house. What is the reason for this precipitous haste?"

"Sidney says—" Dru began, and then a puzzled look flickered over her face. "I do not have to explain anything to you. What do you intend doing with me anyway? We cannot return to London, for it is nearly night and I have been travelling all day." There was a catch in her voice suspiciously like a small sob.

Esme looked to Theo, who said in a soothing voice, "No indeed; we will go to a pleasant inn where you will be very comfortable."

"No, you must have this carriage turned and take me back to Sidney," Dru flared. "You can't make me go to an inn with you. I shall tell the landlord you have kidnapped me and are holding me against my will."

"Your own cousin kidnapping you? Such a thought," Theo said, but with narrowed eyes. "What you both want is a nice cup of tea. We should come to some sort of establishment soon, and then you shall have one."

They were not making as good time on this small side road as they had done previously, but presently, in a small village, they did come to a tiny inn. Theo climbed out of the carriage, and Dru would have followed but, at a nod from his mistress, one of the outriders materialised and blocked the door.

Dru turned on Esme with a passion. "I hate you, Esme Leonardo, and shall never forgive you for this."

"Then I shall have to live with your hatred, Cousin, for I should certainly never be able to live with myself if I let you ruin your life."

"This talk of my ruining myself comes very ill from *you*," Dru said, "when all the world knows that your own mama all but eloped."

"However, she did not," Esme said, her face turned rather white. "She gained Grandpapa's consent and was married quite properly. And if she *had* eloped, the case would not have been the same as yours, for Papa had intended from the start to take her abroad, and he had a means of supporting her in comfort. Whereas you and Mr. Porterfield would have to stay and face the censure of society here in England, since this is where his work is and where he will presumably eventually inherit his brother's title and estate."

Before any more wrangling could ensue, Theo Wild arrived with steaming mugs of tea. For a moment, Dru looked as if she would have refused, but she was really very hungry and thirsty, so she accepted it with a scornful glance. "And perhaps you would like some bread and cheese," Theo offered, opening the hamper. Dru hesitated, but when Theo broke off a bit of bread and cut a piece of cheese and held it out to her, she accepted it sullenly.

They had not been long on the way again before Dru began to nod in her corner. "Miss Channing?" Theo said softly. And, turning to Esme, "Good, we can talk."

Esme looked at her sleeping cousin and listened to her somewhat stertorous breathing. "Good God, have you drugged her?"

The imperturbable Miss Wild nodded matter-of-factly and wrapped Dru's dove grey mantle more closely about her. "It won't hurt her. It will only make her sleep. I questioned the landlord and found that there is a suitable inn some half dozen miles down the road. You must go in and tell the landlord there that you and your cousin were on your way to visit your married sister and expected to arrive before night-fall but that your cousin, who is not a good traveller, felt so unwell that you have had to pause often during the day and now fear to travel on at night. Request a room for the two of you with a truckle bed for your abigail. That sounds a re-spectable enough tale, I think, that we should be able to avoid arousing any undue interest. I will be able to rouse your cousin enough to get her into the place, but I think she will not be alert enough to make any sort of scene."

Esme looked admiringly at Theo Wild. "Yes, I under-stand. That is a good plan."

The landlord at the Black Swan was helpful and sym-pathetic toward Esme's tale, recognising quality when he saw it, not only by her manner and her stylish pelisse, but also by the bang-up rig in which she was travelling.

Between them, they got Dru in bed. Then Theo said, "I

think we can trust that she will not waken, but perhaps it would be better if I ordered some supper brought up here.''

She slipped out of the room and came back shortly, saying, ''The landlord's wife apologises for the simplicity of the fare and offered to cook us up some slices of ham and a meat pie, but I only ordered what was already prepared, as I did not want to waste time having something specially cooked. I am sure you must be as hungry as I.''

When Esme saw the steaming platter of fragrant baked fowl surrounded with vegetables, she thought it was feast enough.

When they had finished and the dishes had been removed, she said to Theo, ''Will we return home tomorrow? What if we have been missed? And with Dru having worked herself up to such a pitch, can we be sure she won't say something indiscreet, or even run away again? And how will we explain our absence?''

''Go to bed now,'' Theo advised, helping her with the fastenings on her dress. ''You must be tired after your long day. I will have to give the matter some thought.''

Though Esme had been sure she would spend the night turning the problem over in her mind, she had time only to utter a prayer of thankfulness that Dru was safely away from Sidney Porterfield and to reflect again upon the strangeness of Theodosia Wild's kind competence before falling asleep.

By the time she awoke in the morning, Theo had already dressed and ordered breakfast brought to their room, not wishing to give Dru the opportunity of making a scene downstairs. Dru still seemed groggy and hardly able to focus her attention, but Theo placed coffee and a plate of warm sugar buns before her and urged her to eat.

''I have devised a plan,'' she said to Esme. ''We are not more than three hours' journey from Exmoreton, and that is where we shall go.''

Esme gave a puzzled frown. ''But what is Exmoreton?''

''That is Honoria Whitechappel's old home, where her

son, the viscount, resides. Locklynde's nephew. I had thought of going directly to Honoria at the dower house, but everyone in London knows you returned from Locklynde Hall only a few days ago. It might be thought eccentric of you to return after so brief a time. I shall send one of my men to fetch Honoria over to Exmoreton and another back to London with letters explaining all to Lady Channing and Locklynde, and an announcement to appear in the *Morning Post* that Miss Channing and Miss Leonardo are paying a visit to Miss Channing's cousin, the Lady Honoria Whitechappel, at Exmoreton. I trust that will silence any speculation about your absence.

"It is tiresome that we can't simply go to the dower house and *say* we are at Exmoreton, but that is the sort of thing one is always being tripped up on. Someone's second parlour maid would be sure to hear from the Whitechappel cook's assistant that there *were* no guests at Exmoreton, and the maid would pass the word along to some lady's dresser, who would tell her mistress and precipitate the very sort of mystery we are trying to avoid."

Suddenly Dru, having drunk up her coffee, aroused from her torpor and stared at Theo. "Good God, it is Theodosia Wild! Esme, why is Jared's mistress acting as your abigail? Are you mad, or am I?"

Unlike Theo, Esme was mortified at Dru's words and flushed deeply. "Miss Wild undertook to help me when I had no one else to turn to. She is acting as abigail in order to protect my reputation and yours."

"Protect our reputations? Theodosia Wild?"

"Exactly," Theo said calmly. "You would neither of you wish to be seen with a high-flier, would you? And you do need a respectable companion. Hence my disguise. Now if you have finished your breakfast, please get dressed so we can be on our way."

"I won't go anywhere with you," Dru said sulkily.

"You will, you know," Theo replied pleasantly. "There is

no hope of Mr. Porterfield's finding you in this out-of-the-way place, and I think you haven't money enough to hire a carriage. Even if you did, where would you go? You don't know where the gentleman may be at the moment. He may still be in that inn, which I doubt you even remember the name of. He might be scouring the countryside, or he may have returned to London. Our main task now is to avoid scandal. Since you have no hope of being reunited with him at present, I'm sure that if you think about it, you will see that this is the best way."

Dru turned to Esme. "I won't go a step with That Woman!"

"Be quiet!" Esme ordered crossly. "It is your fault we find ourselves in this awkward position. You can't suppose Miss Wild *enjoys* careening about the countryside trying to save a gullible green girl from her own folly."

"It is no one's concern but mine, and I don't consider it folly to marry the man I love!" Dru said dramatically.

"Avete torto! In fact, you are quite wrong if you think such clandestine behaviour concerns no one but yourself. Your mother and sisters will feel the mortification strongly, as you well know, or *would* know if you stopped to think of anyone besides your precious Mr. Porterfield. Let us have no more talk. Finish dressing so we can take our leave."

Dru was sullenly silent all the way to Exmoreton. The coachman had to stop once and inquire the way. When they at last turned into the driveway, Esme could see why Lady Honoria preferred to live at Locklynde Hall. The house itself was imposing and rather elegant, but it sat at the base of a rock outcropping and, though there were graceful plantations of trees and shrubs in front and to the sides, the ground was rocky, and nowhere was there a spot which would give full scope to her talents as a landscape gardener.

As they descended from the carriage, Esme said to her cousin, "Will you speak to the butler, or shall I?"

Dru shrugged. "I have nothing to say to him, but I shall have a great deal to say to my cousin the viscount about being brought here against my will."

"Then you will be even more of a gudgeon than I thought. What do you suppose he will have to say if he learns of your disgraceful behaviour? The fewer people who know what has happened, the better for your reputation. If you cannot be sensible, then at least be quiet."

The butler opened the door and, seeing two rather travel-wrinkled but elegantly clad young ladies accompanied by a respectable-looking abigail, ushered them in.

Esme said, "Is the Viscount Whitechappel at home? This is his cousin, Miss Channing, who I am afraid is not feeling quite the thing from the swaying of the carriage. He is not expecting us, owing to a mixup."

"If the young lady would like to sit down, I will see if his lordship is at home."

In a short time, a tall young man with very much the look of his mother around the mouth and nose came into the room. Esme held out her hand. "How good of you to receive us. I am Esme Leonardo, Drusilla's cousin on the distaff side of the family. And this is your cousin Drusilla Channing, your great-uncle Hubert's daughter, you know. I believe the two of you have not met before. I am afraid she has the headache a little from the trip."

The viscount was looking somewhat puzzled, as well he might, and Esme continued with a hopeful smile, "I trust our arrival will not put you out too much, but the case is that your mother invited us to stay with her here for a few days—we were lately visiting at Locklynde Hall—perhaps she wrote you of it?—only due to an unfortunate mishap, we have arrived ahead of her, I fear."

"A mishap? To my mother?" he asked with a worried frown.

"No, no. Nothing of that sort." And because her powers

of invention had for the moment been stretched to the limit, she hurried on quickly, "It is all rather complicated, and she will explain it to you later, but if we could just get Drusilla to a bed where she can lie down and let us bathe her head with vinegar water, I'm sure she'll be better presently."

"Certainly," said the bewildered but courteous viscount, ringing for his butler. "I'm afraid that my wife is away on a short visit just now," he said, which was such a relief to Esme that she burst out, "Splendid!" and, realising the awkwardness of the remark, added, "Splendid that she will not be discommoded by our untimely arrival, I mean."

They were shown to a pretty blue bedroom, and very soon Theo's portmanteaux were brought up. Unfortunately, they did not contain adequate wardrobes, as she had had but little time to pack and had brought them along principally so that it would look as if they were on a legitimate journey if they had to stop for the night.

She had tossed in some nightclothes and undergarments as well as two pairs of kid slippers and two dresses, the first that had come to hand. One was a white jaconet morning dress, the other a black silk taffeta.

Esme had wisely refused the help of a household maid to unpack, saying that her own abigail would attend to it but that if they could have a light nuncheon of some sort brought up on a tray, it would be appreciated.

Now Theo and Esme regarded the contents of the boxes. "I don't quite see how you young ladies are going to dress," Theo said. "You can't stay in those travel clothes forever. Of course, it doesn't matter about me. But what will you do about dinner?"

"I suppose we could say that Dru is too ill to leave her bed and I want to stay with her, but we will eventually have to emerge. I believe the white jaconet would do for Dru if we just pinned the flounce up an inch or so higher, but I am far too short and insignificant for either of them."

"I wish I were an expert seamstress, as a good abigail should be," Theo said.

"Oh, but *I* am," Esme exclaimed. "That is, if you would not mind having your gown altered."

"Not at all; use anything you can find. Perhaps you could contrive some trimming from some of the white lace on one of the night dresses. I do not think unrelieved black is quite your style."

"But it fits my mood," Esme said, though that mood was already lightening at the prospect of having some project to occupy her while they awaited Honoria's arrival. "You *do* think she'll come, don't you?" she asked Theo, "for how I am to face the viscount if she doesn't I can't imagine."

"She'll come," Theo said with assurance. "She is very good in a crisis."

Resolutely, Esme thrust from her mind all thought of how Theo Wild happened to know that Locklynde's sister was good in a crisis. Whatever else might be true, this was no ordinary high-flier. She had been all that was generous with her help, and Esme knew in the recesses of her heart that somehow it was connected with the marquis and her relationship to him. This was not the time to speculate on the nature of that relationship. If she were still Locklynde's mistress—if she truly loved him—then perhaps that was why she had been willing to undertake this vexing project in order to help his cousin.

But if she loved him, then why was she behaving with such extraordinary kindness to that foolish nuisance of a chit, Esme Leonardo? For surely that was the way Theo must have regarded her. Not as a rival—oh no; Esme acknowledged painfully that there was no need for Theo to have thought of her in that way. But surely she must have found it irritating that the marquis had spent so much time with her—time he could have been spending with Theo in the smart little house in Belgrave Square. And yet she had not even read Esme a lecture for her failure to warn Locklynde of Dru's increasing involvement with Sidney Porterfield. She had gone out of her way to protect Esme's reputation as well as Dru's.

It was all a puzzle, and the most puzzling part was that Esme herself could not help liking Theo Wild. She liked her levelheadedness and efficiency. She liked the way she had put everything aside without hesitation to help Esme out of her dilemma. Besides that, she was intelligent and amusing company. Esme thought they might have been real friends under other circumstances.

Her reflexions were interrupted by the appearance of the maid with their nuncheon. They ate bread and butter, and strawberries with cream, and when she came to take the trays away, Esme requested needles and thread.

Dru refused to try on a pair of Theo Wild's kid slippers, but Esme thought they would fit her well enough. On her own small feet, they were much too large. "But they will certainly look better than my half-boots at dinner," she said, "and if I walk with a sort of shuffle like some comic dull-wit in a play, I daresay they will stay on."

"What clever fingers you have," Theo said as she admired the white lace frill that Esme was adding to the décolletage of the black gown. "That looks much more nearly suitable for you now."

"I was thinking," Esme said, "my petticoat has pink satin ribbon run through it. I could take it out and fashion some knots of it for the white dress to make it look a bit more like an evening dress for Dru."

Thus the afternoon passed away with Theo reading aloud from a book of very dull sermons, which was the only volume in the room, making droll comments on some of the more pretentious passages to entertain Esme while she stitched.

It was nearly six o'clock when they heard a commotion in the corridor and then, after a quick tap on the door, Lady Honoria strode in. Ignoring the other two, she went straight to Dru, who was now sitting before a mirror brushing her hair. The girl tried to meet Honoria's eyes defiantly, but as that lady was wearing a darkling look not unlike her brother's when he was in a taking, she could not help quailing a little.

"Well, young lady, a narrow squeak you have had, and I shan't say anything more until your mother arrives, or Locklynde, for one or the other is sure to come and tell you what a thoughtless goose you have been. You can thank fate that Esme and Theo are awake on all suits and have contrived so that you may, with luck, rub through this adventure without scandal."

"Please, ma'am," Esme said, "it was Miss Wild who arranged everything, for I'm sure I should not have known how to manage with Kit away and Lord Locklynde nowhere to be found."

"Well, you couldn't have done better than to place yourself in Theo's hands, though how you—well, never mind. Theo, my dear," she said, stretching out her hand, "I never thought to see you look such a perfect frump."

Theo laughed. "No more did I expect to be one, but it has served its purpose," she said, looking down at her drab brown dress, "for no one has given me a second glance, which I admit is lowering, but useful in this instance."

As Honoria turned back to her cousin, she saw two tears rolling down Dru's cheeks. "Enough of that, child. Stiffen your spine, for dinner is in half an hour. I fear my son thinks it eccentric enough that I have invited you here without a word of warning to him and then failed to arrive before you. I have told him such a tangled tale that I daresay he understood none of it and was glad to have me come to the end of it, but if he sees you weeping into your soup, I cannot imagine what he will think."

The two girls presented a rather unusual appearance in their borrowed gowns, as Esme's was too sophisticated for her and Dru's was scarcely formal enough for evening, though her cousin Honoria had lent her a pink silk shawl that helped somewhat.

Esme was pleased that the viscount took his mother in to the table in front of them since her own peculiar gait, as she tried to keep Theo's slippers on, would have caused him to stare had he had a clear view of it.

Conversation during dinner was a trifle strained, as Dru refused to be drawn out, but Honoria conversed with her son on various topics concerning the estate and their neighbours until at last it was time to withdraw and leave the viscount to his port.

In the morning, Esme's door opened to reveal Theo with a green muslin frock in her hands. "I explained to Honoria that I did not see how you were to leave your room today with nothing to wear but a black silk evening dress. She contributed this if you can take up the hem."

"Oh, how good of her!" Esme cried. "You think of everything."

"Obviously not, or I should have packed with greater care, but time did seem to be more important at that moment, and I suppose I was hoping we could return Dru to her mama that same day, in which case we wouldn't have needed the portmanteaux at all."

"Well, I will start in on hemming this dress immediately," Esme said.

Later in the morning, Honoria announced that she was going to pay calls on several neighbours and wished Dru and Esme to accompany her. "It would look odd if I did not see any old friends while I am here, and besides, Mrs. Talburt has two sisters in London society with whom she corresponds incessantly, so your presence here will be firmly established by the next post."

Dru was very withdrawn and unhappy-looking as they drove away from Exmoreton, but her breeding did not allow her to be discourteous to any of the three neighbours they called on. She was very quiet, but that could easily have been put down to shyness, and Honoria and her friends had enough to talk about to keep up a lively conversation with little help from either of the girls.

"One thing we can be thankful for," Honoria said on the drive home, "is that my daughter-in-law is away on a visit. I do not think she would be so easily fobbed off as my son. I do hope Locklynde will arrive tomorrow or send a message by your mama telling us what to do. I hardly see that we can send you back to town immediately. It would seem much too short a visit to have come so far. And yet I am on tenterhooks lest my son's wife should arrive home and find you here. Your inadequate wardrobes alone would be enough to make her suspicious that some mischief was afoot."

Dru's eyes filled with tears. "Poor Sidney will be frantic wondering what has become of me."

"Somehow I cannot feel any great sympathy for a man who would persuade a young girl to elope, thus making her whole family frantic," Honoria commented.

To that, Esme said a silent amen.

═14═

LADY HONORIA SPENT the afternoon amusing her young grandson and was joined in this occupation by Esme, while Dru retired to her chamber to brood. When the child's nanny fetched him up to the nursery for a nap, Esme decided to go for a walk.

She hardly noticed the grounds through which she was moving, so preoccupied was she by the problems confronting her. She hoped that the morrow would bring at least some word from her Aunt Dora, though she could hardly imagine that good lady organising herself to decide what was to be done with neither her brother nor her son at hand to advise her.

Her heart ached for Dru's unhappiness, but she could not be sorry for what she and Theo Wild had done. Any runaway marriage was to be deplored, but in tying herself to a man so preoccupied with the world's injustice to himself, Dru could only be buying a miserable future. It seemed to Esme that Dru wanted to marry him more to keep him from another disappointment than because she was envisioning a happy life together for the two of them.

After rambling about the estate for an hour, she was just returning across the lawn toward the front door when she heard the clatter of a vehicle coming up the gravel drive. It was a gentleman's curricle, fashionable but built for speed. A footman ran out to hold the horses, and a tall figure—wide of shoulder, thighs bulging under his buckskins, his topboots shining—stepped gracefully down.

Esme could hardly credit her senses. She ran toward him crying, "Jared!" and threw herself against his hard chest. His arms came around her just for an instant before she pulled away in confusion, her heart pounding. "I mean, my lord, I never thought anyone would arrive before tomorrow at the earliest, and I am so very glad to see you because I think you will be most useful in dealing with Dru. We have all been at fiddlesticks' end over what to do with her. She seems not at all prepared to listen to reason."

He studied her face carefully. "My wretched cousin has given you a very bad time, has she?"

"A very worrying time, sir, and I blame myself greatly."

"Well, I think you can absolve yourself of any blame, since you managed to prevent her disastrous marriage."

"I'm afraid, my lord," she said in a small voice, but bravely, "that the credit goes to Miss Wild, for without her I could not have managed."

"Oh, I have learned to count on Theo to be thoroughly efficient," he said, with which she could not but agree, though it did not make her feel as comfortable as it ought to hear him say it.

"What puzzles me," he went on, "is how Theo became involved."

Esme bent her head and seemed to be delivering her discourse to the toe of her shoe. "Well, you see," she said in a rather muffled tone, "when I discovered Dru's note to her mama, I went straight to you—as I should have done when I discovered her meeting Mr. Porterfield in the park on the previous day—"

"I wonder why you did not," he mused. "Go on."

"Your butler said you were not at home and that he had no idea where you were or when you would return. It—it occurred to me that Miss Wild might know, so I went to her."

He gave her a long, penetrating look. "I see. And then?"

"She did not know where you were either, but she saw I was troubled. Somehow I found myself telling her what had happened, and she said Dru must be stopped at all costs. So we set out and kidnapped her from under Mr. Porterfield's nose and brought her here, but now I scarcely know what is to be done with her. She has been a regular watering-pot ever since."

"Poor Esme," he said, smiling a little. "You have had a thin time of it, have you not?"

"Oh, that part doesn't signify, only that I don't know what is to be done, for if she goes back to London, there is no saying she won't run away again. She is quite obsessed with 'poor Sidney.' "

"I think I can manage to quench the fire in her bosom," the marquis said with one of his darkling looks, and despite all that had passed, Esme could not help shivering a little and hoping that he would not be too harsh with Dru.

"Come, let us go into the house and assemble the others."

The first person they saw after the butler had admitted them to the house was the Viscount Whitechappel. He gave a start of surprise. "Uncle, I did not know you were coming. I daresay Mama must have forgotten to tell me." He wore a faint look of alarm, as if wondering by how many more guests this unexpected house party was to increase.

"She was not perfectly sure of my arrival," Locklynde replied. "I'm going to make arrangements to take all this company off your hands, but I shall wish to speak to them privately, Nephew. Could you arrange that we may confer without interruption in the library?"

The viscount appeared bewildered, but Esme thought she had seen some relief in his face when his uncle mentioned taking his visitors away. "Certainly, Uncle."

In a short while, the other three entered the library. His

sister gave Locklynde a kiss; Dru threw him a defiant look, and Theo Wild held out her hand, which he pressed, saying in a low tone, "Thank you, my dear." Then, as he took in her appearance—her hair pulled into a plain bun under a neat cap, her drab gown—his eyes kindled with amusement, and she met them with a look of camaraderie in her own.

Esme averted her glance and fell to studying the tassels on the drapery.

"I know you are going to tell me I ought not to have run away with Sidney," Dru said, the words falling like brittle slivers of ice, "but I think you are the last person to condemn me for—"

"I agree. And I do not intend to comment on your behaviour. I will leave you to draw your own conclusion," the marquis said. "Honoria and Miss Wild know all my history, and I daresay you have heard bits of it, Drusilla. It is true: I was guilty of trying to elope with a young lady, much as Mr. Porterfield did—only, unlike him, I was not clever enough to do it when her brother was safely out of town. He defended his sister and was very nearly killed for his pains. My friends persuaded me to leave England while his life hung in the balance.

"Convinced, quite foolishly, that life without the lady in question was meaningless, I fell into just the sort of excesses a foolish young man of fortune might be expected to do in the capitals of Europe. I think I need not bore you with the details. Then I met an old school friend who was on the ambassador's staff in Vienna. I shall never know why he trusted me with the tale, but he told me that there was a leak of information at the embassy. Someone was selling secrets.

"Being acquainted with the raff and scaff of Europe has its uses: Through some disreputable friends I had made in the seamier establishments I frequented, I was able to get a line on the courier who was carrying secret documents, and he in turn led us to the culprit.

"It was not the last time I was asked to work sub rosa for the embassy. Having tired by now of the aimless life I had been leading, I wanted to come home and buy a pair of colours, but by that time I had contacts with officials in several other of our embassies who convinced me I could be of more use by continuing as I had been doing. The casinos and drinking houses of Europe may seem unlikely places for such business to be carried on, but I assure you they often yield up secrets.

"Theodosia Wild was in a position similar to mine. By that, I do not mean to say that she was frequenting low haunts or anything of that nature. In fact, she was a lady with a considerable fortune, which she had inherited, but she had lost a fiancé and two brothers in the war. The story of how she came to be working for the government is hers to tell, not mine. Suffice it to say that, quite by chance, she stumbled upon some information that proved to be useful in apprehending a traitor. She was asked if she would be willing to continue serving her government in this way. Feeling that she had a bitter score to settle with England's enemies, she agreed.

"She was both brave and clever, and by setting up fashionable salons to which a number of indiscreet young men would flock, she too proved to be of use. We worked together more than once and have kept in touch ever since.

"There was one flagrant case of thievery that we were not able to resolve satisfactorily. Portions of shipments of arms and food sent to our armies abroad were being diverted and sold, much of it doubtless ending up in enemy hands. I had my suspicions but could not find the man's confederates or any solid proof against him.

"When the war was over, I might have abandoned the search for proof except that the man I thought responsible, now out of the army, had been given a government post in the exchequer."

Esme drew in a sharp breath, her eyes widening in shock as she divined the direction Locklynde's tale was taking. Her eyes went to Theo Wild, who was standing easily beside a writing table, one hand resting on its satinwood surface. Somehow even in her dowdy outfit she had a commanding presence, now that she was no longer playing the self-effacing abigail. She was looking at Dru with an expression that smote Esme to the heart as it seemed to be compounded of implacability and pity.

"This man of whom I was speaking," the marquis continued, "has not yet made a great deal of money out of his government post, I think—merely a trifling manipulation of funds here and there and a word in the ear of someone willing to pay for the information about where a dishonest profit could be made, someone with sufficient capital to invest and take advantage of certain prior knowledge. But it was evident that so greedy and dishonest a man must be stopped before he could rise to more important posts where he could do even greater harm. He is the real reason I returned to England. His name is Sidney Porterfield."

Dru's face blanched white, and then a flush rose from her throat up to stain her cheeks. "Oh no, you are mistaken," she cried. "It is just as it always was. You are against him out of spite."

"You are wrong, Cousin." Locklynde's voice was steely. "I am against him because he stole English arms and sold them to the enemy. Theo and I have been working for some time with Sir Wilfred Kenner. We have been building up a case against him for a long time, and at last the final bit of proof we needed seemed to be on the point of falling into our hands. Sir Wilfred sent Theo down to Locklynde Hall with some information I needed, and the case is now complete."

"It isn't true!" There was a sort of desperate eagerness in Dru's voice. "Don't you see—if he cared about money, he would never have eloped with me. I have no fortune, and yet he risked scandal out of love for me. Is this the act of a greedy man?''

The marquis suddenly looked very tired and sad. "Ah, Drusilla, I'm afraid you have mistaken the matter. He knew that I was on his trail. If I should be able to gather enough evidence to prove my case, there would be two options open to him. He could throw up his job and flee the country permanently—which would mean he could never later take possession of his brother's title and estate—or he could marry my cousin out of hand. He took the gamble on you. Don't you see? You were the weapon he thought he held over me. If only he could have married you, could I have brought charges against him—my cousin's husband, my cousin who is sister to my heir?''

Suddenly Dru buried her face in her hands. "No, I don't believe it!''

It was Theo Wild who went to her. "Think back, Drusilla. Was there really a reason for such haste? Porterfield told you he had asked your uncle's permission to address you and that all was hopeless because your uncle wouldn't even answer him. I think you will find that your uncle received no such request from him. Porterfield hoped to tie your cousin's hands by marrying you, but if you want my opinion, Locklynde would not have been swayed by considerations of the honour of his family name. I think he *would* have brought the charges, and you would have found yourself the wife of a proven traitor. So let us have no more talk of not 'forgiving' Esme for sounding the alarm.''

Dru seemed to collapse then. Esme made a move to go to her and then stopped. She ached to put her arms around her cousin, but it was very likely too soon. The wound was too fresh. It would take time before her heart and mind could adjust themselves to the circumstances and she could see her infatuation for Sidney Porterfield for what it was. Until that time came, Esme must figure in her tormented thoughts as the enemy. She could only hope that the day would not be long in coming when Dru could love her again.

It was Honoria who gently led the weeping girl away to her bedchamber.

Esme sadly watched the door close behind them, and then she heard the marquis's voice at her shoulder.

"Come, let us go for a walk," he said in a rallying tone. "Some fresh air would go down very nicely after all the damp emotion we have been subjected to."

Esme turned to Theo. "Will you come?"

Theo looked over the top of Esme's head at the marquis. There was just a hint of a smile about her mouth, but she said gravely, "I think not, child. I am feeling my years and shall sit with my feet up on a cushion and drink a reviving cup of tea"—which surprised Esme because Theo had heretofore seemed quite indefatigable.

The marquis led Esme out the front door, and they strolled in silence for some minutes before Esme said, "Poor Dru. I feel so sorry for her. She was quite convinced Mr. Porterfield was the love of her life, but I hope she is mistaken. She is very young, after all. These English girls seem to have a certain degree of naiveté, do you not agree? Though I suppose it is very charming and considered appropriate by English gentlemen. But I know Dru was attracted to him from the first, and then he made her feel so sorry for him that I think she mistook sympathy for love. Perhaps later she will find a better reason than pity for falling in love."

"Perhaps it is a Channing failing to mistake one's heart the first time around," he said with ironic emphasis. "I certainly did, and so did Kit. You remember the dashing widow? Dru may find that some quiet months in the country will help to mend her heart, and she can make a fresh start next Season."

"I wish she might have cared for Lord Bartling," Esme said. "I think she liked him very well. He is just the sort of husband she needs—sensible and witty and steadfast. I

187

should hope she has had enough of high dramatics to last a lifetime.''

"I believe his regard for her is sincere. Perhaps next year she may find that liking can grow into love. Sometimes even dislike can do so, or at least I like to believe it may.''

Again they walked in silence for some minutes as Esme puzzled over his remark, and then she said, "You told the viscount you were going to take us all away. What do you propose to do with us?''

"Oh, now that you have been seen here at Exmoreton, I think I can safely take you back to Locklynde Hall for a few days. And Theo can return to London. I make no doubt she will be delighted to see the last of the tear-bespattered Drusilla, not to mention the pleasure of getting out of that unbecoming attire she has affected.''

"She was really quite splendid throughout," Esme said generously.

"Yes, she always has been. And since you have become acquainted with her, there is something I should tell you. I make no claims to having been a saint myself, but I do not want any of her *friends* to have the wrong impression of Theo. She was never my mistress.''

Esme's heart suddenly felt curiously light, but she did not know what comment she could make on the subject, so she said, "Well, *è cattivo vento che non è buono per qualcheduno*. It's an ill wind that blows nobody good. At hearing of my visit to your sister at Exmoreton so soon after being at a house party at Locklynde Hall, perhaps Lydia will finally give up hope and accept Wittimore.''

"Ah, this must be some sort of record," the marquis said. "We have been in each other's company for over an hour, and this is the first time you have mentioned *l'affaire* Lydia. But I wouldn't be too sure of her giving up hope on the flimsy evidence that you have been a guest of mine and now of my sister's. I fear there is only one way to deal effectively with the tenacious Miss Milliman. I believe she will never give up until you and I have actually met at the altar."

Esme's heart gave a great leap, but she schooled herself to speak lightly in answer to what was obviously a jesting remark. "Oh, my lord, that seems to be going a step too far. It was a sacrifice for you to pretend an interest in me and attend all those insipid affairs, but even Kit could hardly wish for you to make such a sacrifice as that."

"And yet, at one time, you were willing to sacrifice me to marriage with Lydia herself," he said with a wry face.

"That was before I knew you. Later I came to see that you would not deal together."

"Whereas you and I, Esme, would deal together extremely."

Blood rushed to Esme's cheeks. "Oh, my lord, do not tease me."

"You foolish innocent. Did you really think I was willing to drink lemonade at Almack's all for the sake of deceiving Lydia? If so, you have much mistaken my character."

"I—I do not understand you, sir," Esme said.

"I hardly needed to enter into such a scheme to discourage Lydia. Once I was convinced that she was wrong for Kit, I could simply have forbidden him to offer for her. Since he is my heir, I could have contrived that he obey, no matter how much he feels indebted to his uncle, and if Dora felt uncomfortable accepting a home from Frederick in view of Kit's defection, I could have set her up at Locklynde Hall."

"I *knew* you had a purpose of your own in suggesting that charade!" Esme cried on an exultant note. "And you said it was the milk of human kindness!"

His eyes twinkled as he said with deceptive meekness, "Well, perhaps that was an exaggeration."

"Exaggeration! It was an out-and-out lie. But why did you do it?"

"In the beginning, I thought it would give me a chance to

spend time with your family so I could keep an eye on Dru's unfortunate infatuation with Sidney Porterfield. Then too, if there was any truth to your assertion that Kit was being forced to offer for an unsuitable wife, I thought that, tiresome as his affairs were, I should probably look into it. However, I could have found a less elaborate means to those ends. I believe the real reason I suggested the charade was for the sake of your beautiful eyes.''

Esme's mouth formed an O of astonishment. ''You aren't going to try to tell me that you *wanted* to see more of me! You know you were furious as fire that I had told that lie about our betrothal, and you thought I was wholly unprincipled.''

''Indeed yes, unprincipled but intriguing. And it did not take very long for it to occur to me that a schemer as good as you, who could tell such rappers without turning a hair, was exactly the sort of wife I needed if I should continue trying my hand at uncovering any more plots against the government.''

''I see. A sort of partner in espionage.'' Esme did not sound wholly pleased at his lordship's reason for considering a wife.

''I'm sure you would excel at it. However, I think I may have had my fill of such work and am perhaps ready to settle down to running my estate at last.''

Esme's fingers shredded the petals of a flower she had been holding.

''Then you won't need a partner who can lie well, after all,'' she said in a small voice.

''No, I will not, so you see there is really no need for us to marry—unless you find you can return my love. I hope you can, for I hardly think I can live without you. And *this* time I am sure I know my own heart.''

She cast an incredulous look at him through her thick, dark lashes. ''Do you really mean it?''

The flame in his eyes told her yes as he took her in his

arms; then his eager mouth found her willing lips, and some ecstatic moments later when she had surfaced for air, she was thoroughly convinced that he did.

"Oh, Jared," she cried, "what a good thing I am not a Channing with a propensity for mistaking my heart the first time around. My mama and papa had only one love, and it lasted them a lifetime. I am a Leonardo through and through, and I know it will be just the same with me."